THE

C.J.P. Ionides was one of the
which has never lacked its great originals. After a life spent largely in solitude in the wilds of Tanganyika (present-day Tanzania) he evolved from a great hunter and Game Warden to become a celebrated naturalist, and one of the foremost authorities on poisonous snakes. His knowledge of reptiles, which he collected for museums all over the world, his skill and courage in capturing and handling them, made him famous, but his personal qualities made him one of the outstanding men of his generation.

Margaret Lane spent a long summer in Tanganyika with Ionides, sharing his solitary existence, learning how to catch and handle snakes, and getting to know this extraordinary man. As the days went by she became increasingly engaged by his charm, depth and original thinking. Her story is both serious and light-hearted, an intimate personal view of a man and a country at a turning point. Ionides is a true philosopher and an unforgettable character.

Margaret Lane is a highly regarded writer. Her many books include *The Brontë Story*, *The Tale of Beatrix Potter* and another book about East Africa, *A Calabash of Diamonds*.

HAMISH HAMILTON PAPERBACKS

In preparation

Paul Delany
THE NEO-PAGANS
Friendship and Love in the Rupert Brooke Circle

Nancy Mitford
FREDERICK THE GREAT

Already available

Gerald Hanley
WARRIORS AND STRANGERS

Luigi Barzini
THE ITALIANS

Edward Blishen
A CACK-HANDED WAR

Wilfrid Blunt
THE DREAM KING

For a complete list of available titles please see the end of the book

The Snake Man

BY

MARGARET LANE

A HAMISH HAMILTON PAPERBACK
London

HAMISH HAMILTON LTD

Published by the Penguin Group
27 Wrights Lane, London W8 5TZ, England
Viking Penguin Inc, 40 West 23rd Street, New York, New York 10010, U.S.A.
Penguin Books Australia Ltd, Ringwood, Victoria, Australia
Penguin Books Canada Ltd, 2801 John Street, Markham, Ontario, Canada L3R 1B4
Penguin Books (N.Z.) Ltd, 182-190 Wairau Road, Auckland 10, New Zealand

Penguin Books Ltd, Registered Offices: Harmondsworth, Middlesex, England

First published in Great Britain 1963 by Hamish Hamilton Ltd

First published in this edition 1988 by Hamish Hamilton Ltd

ISBN 0-241-12464-6

Printed and bound by
Cox & Wyman Ltd, Reading

TO

HARRIET

Contents

I

AT HOME IN NEWALA

THE first sounds of morning, long after the frogs had finished and the silence had become total, were disagreeable: no dawn chorus of birds or papery rustle of wind in the banana leaves, but the sudden scrape of a chair on the cement floor, a broom banging the table legs, Makanga's sniffs which were like the tearing of calico, and immediately, as though it had been long held in suspense for these permissive signals, the slow, painful crescendo of Ionides' coughing. I would become aware that it was cold, and the room still in darkness; but gradually the shroud of the mosquito net, hung from the high frame of my bed and enclosing it like a pavilion, would become visible, and the blind windows, blotted out with some colourless material half-felted with dust, would show me the shape of the room and the position of the table. No change of air would tell me that it was morning.

I had come to this place without any clear idea of what I should find, and each day brought its disconcerting surprises. I had first met Ionides two years ago, in London. We had sat out in my garden in the suburban quiet, and he had spoken at length and with distaste of the senseless confusion and noise of civilization. He had seemed like a creature from another world, as indeed he was, sitting in his threadbare clothes and aura of strangeness, with blue eyes warningly alert in his emaciated face, talking of snakes and solitude, and his resolution that never again, never when he once got back there, would he leave Africa. He had lived alone in the bush for thirty-six years, and London shocked him. He made Liwale sound like a mysterious paradise of which he held the secret, and in the course of those long conversations, broken off and continued through a series of curious days, he had developed the notion that one day soon, by the simple expedient of making the necessary journey, I should cast off the tedious confusions of London life and for a time at least, for a visit of perhaps a couple of months or longer, go there too.

Well, here I was; not in Liwale, which he had left in sudden fury a year after our meeting, but in Newala, his new home, in a tin-roofed bungalow plastered like a swallow's nest on the edge of an escarpment, facing south into the clear air and clouds and over a seemingly limitless horizon.

My first thought on getting out of bed, lifting the mosquito net in both hands with care, for it was old and tore easily, was always to unlock the door and step out on the veranda, to taste the day and see what new miracle the light and clouds were working on the distance. It was a majestic prospect of which I never tired; a panorama of endless monotony and variety. Leaning on the wooden rail, one looked down on the tops of a row of banana trees, their huge banners at this hour always weighted down and silvered with the dew; below them the escarpment dropped so steeply that the eye found nothing until it rested on the trees of a further ridge, and below that on the misty thicket of the plain, stretching unbroken for twelve miles or more, where it reached the pewter streak of the Ruvuma. Beyond that ribbon of water lay Mozambique, soft hills and valleys broken by freakish inselbergs of granite which caught the sun and stood up in rosy grandeur like rocks from the sea. It was difficult to believe that life went on under that unbroken covering of bush with scarcely a feature; the eye alone could find nothing to suggest it; but even my small binoculars could pick out the grass roofs of huts among the green, and as far away as the river could distinguish banks of sand and little islands, where wisps of smoke, thin and perpendicular in the windless morning, showed that someone was clearing a patch and burning rubbish. There is in fact widespread cultivation over the whole area, haphazard and invisible; a pocket of millet or cassava, or cashew trees planted around a village, make no impression on the unbroken surface, and the sandy paths which run like a network of thread all over the thicket are covered and swallowed up in the plumy foliage.

This is old slaving country, not more than a hundred miles from the Indian Ocean, the home of tribes who for centuries fed the commerce of the Arab trader, a people depleted by raids yet by no means averse from selling each other into slavery. Not long ago it was all primary forest, but little by little the great trees have been felled and it is now covered by nondescript secondary growth, by tangled scrub and thorny impenetrable thicket. The elephants once inhabiting the forest have withdrawn over the river into Mozambique, crossing only at intervals and by night to raid the crops, and the lions and other big mammals have followed their example. The hippopotamus keeps to the river and it is only occasionally that there is lion trouble. The leopard is still there, and the cautious jackal, but the only indigenous inhabitants to remain in great numbers are the original populations of men and snakes.

This, of course, is the reason why Ionides has come to live there. In the old days, in the years of his fame as a Game Ranger, though the territory under his control included all this country down to the Ruvuma, he rarely came into it, and at one period never set foot in it for eleven years. He is not greatly interested in human beings, and the people in these parts were, at least from his point of view, frequently troublesome. They complained of the depredations of the hippos, but would not build hippo-fences round their crops, preferring to kill the animals when they could and to keep up a continual clamour for him to send his game scouts down to the river to shoot them. They were awkward in exactly the same way about elephants, running mad in the night when they heard the quiet snap and swish of their trunks breaking off the heavy heads of the millet and tossing them into their mouths, and would trap the beasts in pits and attack them with spears, consoling themselves for the loss of grain or cotton with intoxicating feasts of elephant meat and the profits of ivory. As an old elephant hunter, who had known the pleasures of ivory-poaching himself before he had turned respectable, this was intolerable. Like many men who have been great killers in youth, he was now on the elephants' side, and was enraged by slaughter which simple precaution would have made unnecessary, while relatively or totally unmoved by the loss of millet. So after many fierce scenes with the headmen of villages, and failing to bring them round to his way of thinking, he had left the area rather severely alone, only grudgingly sending his African game scouts down to the river when it was patently necessary, and there were rumours of intervention by the District Commissioner.

The area for which he was responsible was so vast, and travel so difficult, that the Makonde Plateau and the steamy lowlands beyond it became, in his individual and prejudiced view, simply not worth while. He solved the problem by leaving a couple of game scouts permanently there, ostensibly under the District Commissioner's orders, but in fact answerable (since they were much more afraid of Ionides) to his own peculiar laws of natural justice. 'The system I worked on was this: the people who pleased me got a certain amount of protection from elephant from the game scouts. Among those who didn't, the elephant were as likely as not to get driven into the cotton.'

And then one day, tracing the Ruvuma River from mouth to source on a tour of inspection, when particularly bitter official complaints had made some personal demonstration necessary, he had come across six green mambas in one day and had thought 'Well!' He had had no idea that these beautiful and dangerous snakes were so plentiful here, and began to pay closer attention to the area. He soon discovered that not only were there mambas hidden in the trees, but that the gaboon viper, of which also he was a collector, was to be found in great numbers in the thicket, and eagerly revised his opinion of the plateau. He had always admired snakes and had a liking for them, and for some years had been sending specimens to the Coryndon Museum at Nairobi and even an occasional live one to the London Zoo, and he now saw this exasperating area in a new light, as territory which would be well worth visiting from time to time in his own interest. Accordingly, when he retired from the Tanganyika Game Department in 1956 and settled at Liwale, rejoicing in the prospect of leisure for his special pursuits, he made frequent safaris south into the Makonde country, hunting for snakes; and when a particularly flagrant act of trespass had finally disenchanted him with his new home (he had returned from a long safari in Kenya to find that an African neighbour had cut down his trees in his absence and planted some sort of food crop all over the garden) he had shaken the dust of Liwale from his feet in a rage and gone cursing south, to the brink of the Makonde Plateau, where he knew that the snakes and hoped that the people would prove better neighbours.

He had been at Newala a year when I arrived, and had certainly found the snakes up to expectation. They abounded, and he responded with a passionate concentration. He was now past sixty, and though a little deaf, owing to a mishap with a shotgun and another with an elephant, still remarkably hard and muscular in spite of the starved elegance of his appearance. But there had been another accident of an unexpected sort: in the year of his retirement he had been stricken with a painful thrombosis of the right leg, which had meant a weary journey to England and some months in hospital; and though he refused to be over-cautious he was fully aware that his activities were limited. Henceforth he would concentrate on his beloved snakes, which, despite many lurid legends to the contrary, move neither fast nor far, and can be caught by a man who can walk half a mile through the bush and has the comfort of a Land Rover. For the rest, for any enterprise which involved distances through thicket or swamp where a vehicle could not go, he had provided himself with a little bush-cart on poles, supported on a single wheel, in which he could be piloted quickly and easily by a couple of bearers.

I had had, I think, vague visions of long journeys which we would undertake together, poking about in swamps in search of pythons and keeping an alert eye for any furtive hint of movement in the high branches; the last thing I had been prepared for was the monastic rule of enclosure under which I now lived, cooped up with him at close quarters in this dark dwelling, from which we emerged only at certain hours into the sunlight, like snakes from a hole.

The journey itself had fed the mounting sense of expectation, for the aeroplane from Dar-es-Salaam had been small and had flown at no great altitude over long sweeps of coast and the turquoise and aquamarine of the Indian Ocean, where scattered necklaces of islands, some piercing the surface with coral rock and beaches, some still unborn, awash with weed and breakers, plotted our course with a chain of coloured fragments. We had come down on the air-strip on Mafia, the largest of these islands, and while boxes of freight were unloaded I had had time to admire the groves of coconut palms, and to hear the continuous distant drone of the reef. When the plane had taken off the shadow of its wings had rushed violently over the turf and great grasshoppers had sprayed out from it in alarm, visibly spreading their wings in the sudden gale. Nachingwea was the end of the run, the last air-strip; and I had a momentary feeling of panic lest Ionides should not, after all, be there. But there he was, courteously punctual and precise beside his Land Rover; and within minutes we were sitting together with the African driver, raising a cloud of orange dust over the slow monotonous seventy miles that ended at Newala.

The house, when we lurched finally over the sandy path at the back of it, scattering chickens, looked commonplace enough, if a little dilapidated; it was not until I was led round to the front, to the veranda, that the huge airy distance suddenly opened, and I found myself on the edge of a dizzy drop. The door creaked and I was ceremoniously shown into the gloomy interior.

I had been long expected, and the smiling African who carried my luggage into the room and through a short passage did so with the conscious air of one who has spent many hours in preparation. I followed him into a dark and roomy chamber, where a dripping bowl of hot water had been placed on the dressing-table, and where I was discreetly left to wash and unpack, and make myself at home.

My first move was to go to the windows for the sake of a little light, but it appeared that they had not been made to open, and the glass, coated with dust and patterned with the courses of old rains, was further obscured by curtains of stuff drawn tight across the panes and nailed into position. The room had a second door, leading to the veranda, but there was giggling and whispering outside and a shuffling of bare feet, and I preferred to leave it closed. Instead I prised one of the curtains loose and pulled it aside, so that I could take stock of my new home and arrange my belongings.

There were two beds in the room, one with a pavilion-like frame of rough wood above it, swathed in mosquito netting, the other with nothing but a stout mattress, evidently not intended to be used. The veiled bed, when I parted the netting and looked in, was tousled and unmade; it looked as though it had been slept in for some time by a person of vigorous habits. Apart from the beds there were two big bookcases in the room, a table under a stained cloth, and a dressing-table with drawers in it, all evidently put together by an African carpenter using some local wood. There was also a wooden chair but no cupboard, and when I cautiously moved the wash-basin and opened the drawers I found them stuffed full of a tangled assortment of clothes, unwashed socks, old razor-blades, handkerchiefs, rags and empty cigarette packets. There was nowhere to put my clothes, which fortunately were few, not even a nail on the back of the door and only one in the wall, precariously maintaining its hold in the crumbling plaster. The floor, which at first I took to be the earth but which was really cement mixed with the local copper-coloured sand, had not been swept for a long time and the corners were plentifully strewn with spent matches. The bookshelves were full of interesting-looking books, all thick with dust, the spines of some of them laced together with cobwebs; one would say that they had stood untouched for years, and that the room had been long abandoned. It was not for some time that I realized that Ionides, with a host's courtesy, had vacated it in my favour the day before, and that this bedroom was his own.

Alone in the living-room, in a haze of cigarette smoke and with his feet on the table, he was patiently waiting for the moment when the conversation begun in the Land Rover could be resumed. This had been more of a monologue than an exchange, for I had been choked by the dust rising at every pot-hole from the floor-boards and had not yet learned the trick of shouting in his right ear so as to be heard above the noise of the engine, the unnerving clatter of miscellaneous gear and the chatter of a knot of Africans in the back of the vehicle. From time to time Ionides would turn his head with great suddenness, presenting to the passengers a glittering eye and a predatory profile, and would yell one menacing word at them in Swahili, which silenced them for a while. But not for long.

Some peculiarly violent crash would throw them all together and set them laughing, and the cheerful din would continue as before. The conversation, if his one-sided communications could be called such, had been chiefly, I remember, to do with the military exploits of the early Mongols, a subject of which I knew nothing (though I was to be well instructed in the weeks to come), and since I could think of no replies worth making I had nodded and smiled my way over seventy miles while keeping a steadying grip on the smaller luggage.

We now had the afternoon before us, and he removed his feet from the table and stood up with a welcoming smile and vaguely bowing gesture, inviting me to the heavy chair at his side. His appearance and behaviour are both romantic and singular; authority and courtesy, ferocity and gentleness combine in a manner peculiar to himself, and irresistible. John Gunther, who met him some years ago in Dar-es-Salaam, aptly described him as looking like a faun, and indeed I have never seen anyone who is in the least like him. The profile is indeed notably satyric; fierce eyebrows, an extremely mobile mouth which curls at the corners, an archaic nose curving outward and suddenly down, give him the appearance, seen from the side and in repose, of an emaciated and aristocratic goat. But his face is rarely in repose except when he is alone. The blue eyes blaze with animation, he smiles often, the expression of close attention is habitual, and everything he does, even listening, is performed with the very essence of concentration. He is a marvellous talker, and his listening is as eloquent as his speech; I doubt if anyone has a keener appetite for conversation.

Genghis Khan, however, and his Mongol hordes, which he was eager to pursue, fell foul of a domestic interruption. I presently asked if one of the dressing-table drawers might conveniently be cleared, so that I could unpack a little, and the realization dawned with furious suddenness that in spite of his orders of the day before nothing whatever had been done. He drew a breath, then checked himself, said 'Excuse me' with a courteous inclination of the head, and let out a yell of such volume that I blenched. There succeeded a silence in which we both listened, I with my nerves tingling, Ionides with the quivering intensity of a lion which has just roared and is weighing the advisability of doing so again; and presently a door opened with a long creak and the house-boy who had carried my luggage appeared, mildly inquiring, with an open and childish gentleness of expression, what more we might require.

Ionides now rose with ominous slowness and stalked into the bedroom, whence I heard an explosion of wrath in what I judged to be extremely eloquent Swahili, punctuated by Makanga's grunts of effort as he began to drag the dirty sheets from the bed. It had never occurred to him that his explicit orders might not have been carried out, and he had naturally made no inspection. Nor, I suspect, had he the remotest idea of what should, or should not, be done. Such knowledge, like the implementing of it, was his servants' business. He employs eight, all told, for the comfortable running of his household, and since he not unreasonably expects never to do a hand's turn himself, regards the giving of orders and the paying of wages as the end of his obligation in the matter. Now he was angry, and when I followed with appeasing protests found him bent on extorting retribution. Would I kindly mention, now and at all times, whatever I wished to have done? He presumed that I spoke Swahili well enough for such menial purposes, and when he found that I did not, swallowed his surprise, and with a controlled distaste showing only in the slight lift of his upper lip, gave instructions that all conceivable personal services were to be performed instantly. Would I, for instance, care to have my shoes cleaned? I said I would, for they were thick with dust, and I guessed that some symbolic action was desirable. I removed them accordingly and started to grope in my canvas bag for sandals while Makanga, with a laborious parade of keenness and efficiency, snatched them up and took them to the dressing-table. I watched his operations out of the corner of my eye while he ferreted in the book-case for a rag (there appeared to be a supply behind the books) and, breathing heavily, held the shoes at arm's length over my clothing and beat the dust off them.

By this Ionides was seemingly pacified, and returned growling to the other room, where he sank into his deck chair, drew a packet of cigarettes from his pocket, and with murmured comments both in English and Swahili prepared to observe the spectacle of Makanga's activity. A broom was fetched, and the cement floor brushed so vigorously that a cloud of dust softly advanced up the passage and invaded the living-room. A cardboard box was carried through and presently returned, full of miscellaneous rubbish; an empty gin bottle, under our silent gaze, was filled with water and conspicuously carried in; Ionides' clothes were removed in bedraggled armfuls, all to the accompaniment of heavy grunts to mark the undertaking's onerous character.

This was the beginning of a series of mild changes in the domestic arrangements which, as we got to know one another better and I discovered that in this respect if not in all Ionides was the least touchy of men, furnished us with continuous amusement. I was extremely cautious in suggestions for my own comfort, for it was only too apparent that I had broken in on a way of life which had been long established, and I shrank from imposing alien ideas. Still, I was pressed, with a courteous and even scientific interest, to mention any ameliorations that occurred to me, and the few that I named, as likely to contribute to the general comfort, were speedily attended to. My bedroom was never swept again, to my relief, the dust being very much better left where it was; but the household refuse, commonly thrown at random from the end of the veranda, was removed elsewhere, and the rough strip of grass by the banana palms, which was the only level ground for sitting out of doors, was raked clear of rusty tins, spent batteries and other detritus. This, I think, with one exception, was the full extent of the domestic revolution; but it was radical; and Ionides protested often that Makanga and the house were both transformed and would never be the same again.

'I'm thinking of changing the name of the house to Hygiene Hall,' he told Norman Horsley, the Game Warden from Nachingwea, who dropped in one day with his lorry and game scouts and stayed to eat all the available bread and butter before moving on: 'you've no idea of the revolutionary changes. It reminds one of *Julius Caesar*—lionesses whelping in the streets, graves yawning, rooms being swept, grass cut, rubbish removed, all phenomena against nature. The *bath*, Norman, has been *cleaned*.' (This was true. The bath, which was in a sort of condemned cell with a high window, cemented against a dirty wall and so heavily ringed with layers of unidentifiable deposits that in the gloom I could not tell what it was made of, had actually, after my first bath, been scoured, and proved to be of ordinary white enamel.) All this was said with an air of exaggerated politeness and that expression of malevolent glee of which Ionides is a master; but Norman Horsley took it *au sérieux* and was not diverted. 'That's the trouble with women,' he said; 'they ruin Africa.'

I could see that this was true, and made a mental note that I had better be careful. But in fact I need not have worried, for though he was himself wholly indifferent to a degree of dirt, bad food and superficial squalor, Ionides showed a generous anxiety for my comfort, and found it amusing to watch Makanga's attempts to understand and fall in with my foreign ways, and the eloquent pantomime of his mystification.

The food, as I quickly learned, was going to be a difficulty, for Ionides is almost exclusively carnivorous and I am not; our habits of eating could hardly be more dissimilar. His diet never varies; the three meals of the day are always the same. For breakfast he has a single sausage and a cup of diluted coffee essence; for luncheon a lump of goat's meat, roasted by some unknown process to the colour and consistency of a motor tyre, at which he patiently saws throughout the week, mashing such fragments as he is able to detach, after much labour, with a boiled potato and a teacupful of some dark and viscid substance described as gravy. For supper some tinned cheese is melted and poured on a slice of bread, followed by another dose of coffee essence sweetened with four teaspoonsful of sugar. The very thought of vegetables fills him with disgust, which is perhaps fortunate, since in this district very few are obtainable.

At the first breakfast I had asked for tea; it arrived in a grimy enamel teapot but proved to be coffee, so astonishingly nasty that I was moved to ask what brand of essence he used. He said he did not know; his cook had orders to buy a particular sort which came in bulk in containers convenient for packing the smaller snakes. The sausages (this was the end of the week) were high, and I went without, and was ashamed to find the goat's meat also unmanageable. However, the problem was quickly and obligingly solved, though Ionides said at first, in answer to my faint inquiries about fruit and vegetables, that none were to be had. This was not true; he had simply never troubled to inquire, having no use for them himself; but quite enough for my needs could be obtained locally. There were papaya trees in the neighbourhood and delicious limes, and a half papaya, its black seeds scooped out and the juice of a lime squeezed over the coral flesh, became my invariable breakfast. Some of the natives grew tomatoes which could be bought in the village, where they were spread on the ground in the market-place; onions came in by lorry from the coast and were to be found at the Indian trader's, and a little egg-plant called a *brinjal* accompanied my daily salad of onion and tomatoes. There were, besides, small green bananas which were quite good, and which Ionides with close attention watched me eat, as though he were studying the feeding habits of a reptile. He never ceased to be amazed that I could consume such things, and raw into the bargain, and would go back to the mastication of his rubber goat with a sigh and a shake of the head, as who should say, one is never too old to learn. The only one of my meals which did not shock him was my supper, which was always, after the first day, two fried eggs with bread. It was not his taste, but at least it did not alarm him for my safety, like the disgusting vegetables.

One always ate from battered enamel plates, chipped and discoloured by unimaginable uses long before he had acquired them with the house; apart from odd teacups and a few saucers there was no china, and I discovered that he considered the use of china plates, for a bachelor, a symptom of effeminacy. The goat was brought to the table in an enamel pie-dish, in which it had to be held at both ends by Makanga during the unusually strenuous operation of carving. The dishes were washed in a bucket at the back door and stacked on a shelf in a sort of general scullery at the back, where the jars of pickled snakes were kept and the live chameleons, together with piles of boxes and sacking over which enormous cockroaches hunted after dark, scampering away when one passed with a lantern on the way to the lavatory. The arrangement looked confused but had its virtues; it was always comparatively easy to find anything.

It was all, in fact, perfectly comfortable once one had got used to it, and after the first two days I could not remember why I had found it depressing. The bed was good, one had a generous two buckets of water to bathe in daily; there was a fire at night when the temperature dropped and the evening wind was cold; the solitude and quiet were absolute. I made only one further tentative suggestion, which had to do with the washing of the tablecloth. This long-suffering object, like the furniture and the enamel plates and indeed practically everything except

Ionides' own deck chair and writing table, had been bought with the house; it permanently covered the table at which we ate, and was never removed, brushed, shaken or otherwise refreshed in the course of its unremitting duties. Food was spilt on it, boxes of snakes, shedding dust and grit, were placed on it for inspection, chameleons were packed into bags on it on Sunday mornings, and it had long ago arrived at a condition which, however hungry one might be, had an inhibiting effect on appetite.

At about the end of the first week I asked Ionides, with apologies, whether it might be washed, and was met with the usual courteous response, as to a surprising but admittedly interesting notion which was worth trying. Makanga was bellowed for (I had jumped so uncontrollably at these sudden yells that they were now considerately prefaced with a polite 'Excuse me, I am going to ring my bell') and the project was explained to him in Swahili. He took it well, lifting the cloth by the corners and examining the stains, but the conversation went on for a long time, covering, apparently, the enumeration and discussion of objections. Eventually the cloth was removed and Ionides translated. 'He is willing to wash the cloth, but wishes to point out that it will not be the slightest use, the stains you complain of being due to bats' urine, which, as everyone knows, are impossible to remove.' This was something outside my experience, but Makanga was right; the cloth, freshly washed and ironed, displayed as before a complex of yellowish maps, and *mkojoo wa popo*, the cause of the trouble, was established between us as the perfect unanswerable excuse for all shortcomings.

II

ON THE MAKONDE PLATEAU

CATCHING snakes is not like any other kind of hunting, and the visions I had of following Ionides through swamp and thicket, pursuing trails and uncovering hiding-places, like most of the preconceptions of ignorance were without substance. Snakes are seen more by accident than design, and to capture numbers of them daily, as he does, depends on an organized system of information. At some time during each day in the dry season, in any number of places and at varying distances from the still centre where he lies in wait, snakes will be seen by chance by a number of people, and until there is news of the quarry he will not stir. By a strange provision of nature it arrives hot-foot every morning except Sundays, usually early; by half-past nine, when Rashidi the head snake-hand makes his report, Ionides, who for the past two hours has been lying supine in his chair, apparently meditating, springs suddenly to life, and without delay the cavalcade sets forth.

By this time the news-bearers, an average of anything up to half a dozen, will have walked, bicycled, or thumbed a ride in a lorry from their villages, and these all now pile into the back of the Land Rover with the two snake-hands, a cumbrous assortment ofboxes and catching gear, and the exceedingly tall, thin, silent and impassive African whom Ionides employs as a driver. Each of the news-bearers will have left a colleague, usually a boy or financially interested neighbour, at the spot where the snake was seen, in order to watch it, for reptiles are marvellously adept at disappearing and nothing annoys Ionides more than to waste time and petrol on a fool's errand. The news is never brought to him personally; if it is he will not receive it; the proper channel is through Rashidi, who decides when a sufficient number of scouts has arrived and comes to the door at last to inform his master.

Snakes are notoriously difficult to see, but Africans have sharp eyes, and on no single day during the month I spent at Newala (except Sundays, which are set aside for snake-packing) was there any lack of them. A man raking up branches while clearing a patch of bush for cultivation, a woman gathering firewood, a child attracted by a commotion of birds in a tree, will catch sight of a moving ribbon among the leaves, or will hear a hissing; and because authentic snake-news is profitable will set about relaying it, often over a considerable distance, instead of setting up a hue and cry and killing the snake, as they did before Ionides came into the district. His activities, which have acquired the importance and dignity of a local industry, have brought about a notable change of heart in this respect, and villagers who in the past felt only traditional terrors in the presence of snakes, now regard any likely specimen with a covetous eye, as something for money.

The Makonde people, being avaricious (or, as the African District Commissioner put it to me more delicately, 'very sensitive about money'), are willing to go to considerable trouble as news-bearers. Unlike the Mafia tribes whom we encountered later, who regard money with indifference and can only intermittently be induced to work for it, they will overcome even their indolence for a few shillings, so that we often set out in the morning with men who had walked through the bush for a good many miles. Each species that Ionides collects has its regular price, which is paid only after the capture; he is too old a hand to pay for something which has unaccountably vanished by the time he arrives, no matter how lively the messenger's pantomime of astonishment. On such occasions he walks coldly away without listening to explanations, climbing back into the Land Rover with an expression of such scornful and long-suffering patience as to leave even the arrogant crestfallen. Nor will he touch a snake which has been in any way tampered with; if he suspects that it has been touched or moved, if the finder has gone to the trouble of digging a trench round it or has temporarily imprisoned it under a basket, he will stop short, utter an imprecation in Swahili and turn on his heel with such an air of menace that children are snatched into safety out of his path. His reasons for this severity are practical: if anyone who has a mind to it is going to experiment with handling dangerous snakes (and these people on occasion are heavy drinkers) sooner or later someone is going to be killed. If snakes are to be restrained by inexpert hands, driven into sacks, pushed into rubbish pits, poked into baskets, they are likely to get damaged in the process and good specimens will be lost, a calamity which he regards as more regrettable than some interfering know-all getting bitten. Besides, he *likes* catching snakes; they are the mainspring of his curious existence, and he has the adept's hostility to all profane and foolhardy interference.

When the rules are kept, and the snake is successfully caught and put into its box, he pays generously; for gaboon vipers, black-and-white cobras and black mambas twenty shillings a snake, for green mambas five, and two shillings each for boomslangs and spitting-cobras. He often disburses as much as ten pounds in a morning, passing the notes in silence to Rashidi, who as silently presses them into the outstretched hand. No word of thanks is spoken on either side, conventional expressions of gratitude not being customary with these people, who preserve a devout decorum in the presence of money.

They all believe that Ionides is a rich man who has made a fortune out of his snake-collecting, which is very far from the truth; museums and zoos cannot afford big prices, and the costs of his collecting (two drivers, two snake-hands, a Land Rover and a lorry), together with occasional long safaris into Kenya, are so heavy that he pursues his trade as a luxury and at considerable loss. His modest private means and his pension from the Game Department enable him to live as he chooses, which is all he asks; he is always nettled by the first question every African puts to him about snakes—'How much money can you make out of them?' Still, he has reason to be glad of the prevailing avarice, for without the profit motive his precious snakes would be slaughtered as before, and he could do nothing.

At the end of a morning's snake-catching as many as eight or nine gaboon vipers—handsome, heavy snakes, as thick as a man's arm—will be wreathing about in their boxes in the Land Rover, a green mamba or two will be exploring the dark interiors of calico bags, nailed down for safety into smaller containers, messengers will have been dropped off one by one after each catch, and the dusty vehicle, smelling very strong by this time, when the sun is hot and all of us happily sweating, sets off on its clattering journey back to base. Mustapha the driver is skilful and careful, but the roads are deep in sand and full of holes, the bush paths overhung with thorns which scrape us as we pass, the hard tracks broken with eroded gullies, so that the boxes and metal grab-sticks leap and crash as we lurch along, breathing the dust which rises from every crevice and settles softly into our hair and clothing. Once back at the house the boxes are carried briskly into the living-room and the snakes sorted out into the quarters they will inhabit for the rest of the week. The mambas, too active and dangerous to be good company, are stacked in their nailed-up boxes in the far corner, where they subside into the philosophic coma which carries them through to their final destination; the gaboon vipers and puff-adders, lethargic by day and seemingly quite indifferent to captivity, are transferred into wire-fronted boxes and stacked like expanding bookshelves against the wall, within a few inches of our chairs. For the rest of the day, and for every afternoon and evening until the following Sunday, we and the snakes, mutually observant, will keep one another company. They are quiet companions for the most part and settle down at once, becoming active only occasionally in the evenings, when they move about their cages, exploring the wire mesh with flickering tongues, staring with jewelled eyes into the lamplight.

Any visiting Africans who call from time to time to see the snakes (for Ionides' fame has given his house the charm of a weird sideshow) never fail to express a delighted horror at their closeness, nervously choosing chairs at the far side of the table and protesting, with much laughter and politeness, that they cannot imagine how anyone can live and eat in the same room. But in fact the snakes are far from disagreeable company, and each day reveals some unsuspected beauty. Ionides silently contemplates them for hours; the least sound or movement from the boxes draws his eyes at once with pleasure and interest. I soon found them as entertaining as he did, and my habitual chair, at no more than arm's length from the wire, an almost perfect position for observation. They smelt very little, and with only one exception not unpleasantly; one missed them quite surprisingly on Sundays, when the boxes stood empty and the week's catch had been packed ready for its journey by lorry to the air-strip at Nachingwea.

Monday morning had always the feeling of renewal, when the blankness of Sunday was over and one could begin afresh. The road to the village would already be busy with people, all walking softly barefoot through the sand, the women bright as butterflies in their gaudy *kangas*, a baby on each back, a burden beautifully balanced on each head. The Makonde men have the reputation of treating their wives well, and in the matter of simple finery they are certainly generous, for a pair of cotton *kangas* never costs less than twelve shillings* (one draped round the body, one hanging in elegant folds like a veil from the head) and all the women and girls have a sumptuous appearance. Their skins are glossy and their cotton draperies in every brilliant and emphatic colour and design, with the further embellishment of mottoes of an improving nature printed in Swahili round the borders; the contrast of darkness and brilliance is extremely exotic. (The mottoes, now so fashionable that it is impossible to buy a *kanga* free from the sort of sentiment that one used to find worked in cross-stitch in cottage parlours, were originally the speciality of prostitutes, who favoured distinctive slogans on their garments such as 'Come, sir, I am ready', and other less translatable invitations; but this provocative fashion has been bowdlerized, and all the mottoes that I could get Ionides to interpret were unexceptionable—'The good name of the children is the parents' glory' being a fair specimen.)

The Makonde women have a notable carriage even by African standards, for until 1957 the plateau was as dry as a bone and they had to walk many miles to fetch water. There is not a single stream or well in the whole area, which supports about two hundred thousand people. The springs are all at the foot of the escarpment, and a lifetime of carrying heavy water-pots on the head over long distances and up and down the precipitous paths of the cliff has given them a majestic confidence of movement. The distances are now much less since a Government water scheme, financed by a Bank of England loan, was put into operation; the water is pumped up by a power station at Makote into huge tanks and piped all over the plateau to locked water points, where the people attend at certain hours to buy their meagre ration at a halfpenny a gallon. This makes it, they say, the most expensive water in the

* In 1871, when Stanley first saw and described these simple garments, they cost three shillings, and he records that complaints were bitter about the price.

world, and certainly they are poor and can afford to use very little. Many of those who live near the edge of the escarpment still make the laborious descent to the spring where water is free, and the scheme, which runs at a loss, could supply three times the number of people who make use of it. It is an old grievance and an old problem, for these are a clean people who love to wash themselves and their clothes as often as possible; but halfpennies are scarce and women not absolutely tireless, so water is here the greatest of all luxuries.

It seems curious that the Makonde have preferred to inhabit the plateau rather than the plain, where streams gush out from the rock even in the dry season, and if you question them they will reply with a myth which carries small conviction. The first man, they say, the black Adam of these parts, settled with his wife in the fertile valley near the water, but when their first child was born it sickened and died. When a second child had been lost they consulted the spirits, and received the evidently sound advice that they should move to higher ground, where they have lived and multiplied happily ever since. The more knowing among them, if pressed, will smile at this story and explain that the soil of the plateau is better than the soil in the valley, adding, if they are men and therefore exempt from water-carrying, 'We like to have food in plenty and go far for our water rather than sit by the stream and starve.' But not even this explanation is convincing, for in a droughty season crops on the plateau fail and there is famine, while in the steamy heat below they flourish and ripen. The truth of the matter is probably that the high ground, though dry, is cool and healthy; there is a strong wind morning and evening and even in the rains, when the heat is hardest to bear, it is not insupportable; while the plain a thousand feet below suffocates with heat, is laborious to cultivate, and malarial.

Several distinct tribes inhabit the plateau, but the Makonde are by far the most numerous. They were all warriors once, before centuries of slaving had culled the stock and the prohibitions of progress overtaken them, and they are still on the whole a handsome and cheerful people. The line of their lower jaw is long and slender, giving the face something of the wedge-shaped elegance of a Siamese cat's; the pupil of the eye is almost black, set in a white so unblemished and opaque that the eyes have a sort of expressionless perfection, like those made of lapis and chalcedony which stare from the lids of Egyptian mummy-cases. The weakest feature is often the chin, and for this reason the most strikingly handsome men, of which there are a few, are those who succeed in growing a little beard.

Many of the women adorn themselves with a criss-crossing of scars on cheeks and breasts, which in the glossy skin has almost the effect of raised needlework, and is curiously attractive. They are fond of ear-rings and beads, and those little gilt studs and rings which they buy from any of the Indian stores, and wear in a pierced nostril. But their most sensational ornament—if indeed it is such, and not, as they claim, a deliberate disfigurement—is the *ndonya* or lip-plug, round which a hole in the upper lip is gradually stretched until the woman's mouth is wholly concealed and the lip can accommodate a cylinder as large as a tea-cup. The effect is monstrous in the extreme, fully justifying the name of duck-bill, and so hideous to western eyes that the Makonde must have grown tired of answering travellers' and missionaries' questions about this mutilation. The answer is always the same: in the old days it was done to make the women unattractive to slave-raiders, and the practice has continued to the present day. I am not sure that I believe this; the Zanzibar slave market, sole channel for the export trade in this part of East Africa, was closed by treaty with the Sultan in 1873, nearly a hundred years ago, yet plugs of different sorts and sizes are still in use by at least three tribes, which would suggest that it is a matter of fashion rather than defence. It is true that all the duck-billed women one sees nowadays are middle-aged or old, the younger ones having abandoned the practice, but their own attitude to the freak is one not of horror but of admiration, and they speak of it as being their *enzi*, which means their glory. There are a thousand forms of mutilation to be found in Africa, as among most primitive peoples, and most if not all are done for motives of sexual attraction, for magic, or simply for fashion. The lip-plug is not to our taste, but I suspect it once had an air of great *chic* to the Makonde, and that it is not so much the suppression of the slave trade as contact with the west that is putting an end to it. The Makua women, who originally came from Mozambique and live around Nanguruwe, 'the place of pigs', where Ionides catches some of his biggest vipers, wear a small black plug like a button in the upper lip, which looks not undistinguished; while the Mawia, who come across the Ruvuma from Portuguese territory, wear a large plug with a spike in it which has a truly horrendous appearance, suggesting remote cousinship with the rhinoceros; but to an eye from another planet they would perhaps seem no more strange than high-heeled shoes, and I fancy they are simply an exotic traditional fashion.

As in most parts of Africa where the white man's rule and the missionaries have had a long innings, primitive beliefs and virtues are in decline. The tribes no longer live under hereditary chiefs, and Islam, which came in with the Arab trader, and to a lesser degree Christianity, have weakened the magical hold of the old religion. There are still a few old people living who remember the Maji-Maji rebellion of 1905, which germinated in the belief that water from the hot springs near Liwale would, if sprinkled on the warriors and their spears, make them immune from German bullets and so free them from the white oppressors who at that time administered the territory. Rebellion is perhaps hardly the word to use for this uprising, which spread with magical rapidity from tribe to tribe and gave birth to what the German Governor, Von Götzen, described as 'a phenomenon quite new in the East African negro—a complete contempt for death in battle'. It assumed, in fact, with a hundred thousand square miles of Africa in revolt, the dimensions of a national war of independence, and the witch-doctors who dispensed the drops to turn the enemies' bullets into water were regarded as intermediaries of a divine power. Nothing but total faith in the efficacy of the magic could have put heart into so hopeless an enterprise, for the Germans met it from the beginning with efficacious brutality, and thousands of men and women were beaten, shot, hanged, and otherwise put to death with ignominy and torture. Yet the insurrection went on, and no failure of the magic seemed to bring any diminution of faith. Once the water had been drunk and drops ceremonially sprinkled on their bodies and weapons, the warriors knew themselves to be immortal, and devoutly accepted the witch-doctors' explanations of the numerous dead. Each warrior who fell had broken one of the rules on which the magic depended, must have made a mistake in the code by which various things were called by misleading names—a lion must be spoken of only as a sheep, Europeans as 'red earth', soldiers as moths, and so on—or, most likely of all, had disobeyed the first injunction of the medicine and had intercourse with a woman. There was no question of recantation, even in defeat, and the old men who still remember the Maji-Maji no doubt prefer to believe, not that the magic was illusory, but that some fatal disobedience betrayed the fetish. But fanatical propaganda of this sort would meet with small response today, and though desire is strong to see the last European leave, ambition is set on following the western pattern.

Ionides has lived more than half his life in Tanganyika and mourns for the old virtues, as old men do. These used, he says, to be a hardy people, who could travel long distances on foot and endure great hunger and thirst without complaint; whereas now, 'that revolting expression, "improving their standard of living"', is emasculating them and making them soft, so that a man cannot travel a dozen miles without a lift in a lorry. For this, being a passionate reactionary, he blames 'progress', a word he cannot pronounce without a backward jerk of the head and his moustache rising in scorn under his nose; but he is opposed to change of every sort and prefers not to hear of it, being fond of comparing the behaviour of human beings, to its discredit, with the greater reserve and dignity of other animals.

It was for this reason, or so he said, that he refused to go with me one Sunday when I drove twelve miles to Mahuta to see the stilt-dancers. There is no native art to speak of in these parts, no music or carving or decorative crafts (though they make good baskets), and the stilt-dancing of Mahuta is a curious survival. It demands both skill and training, for the dancers perform on stilts about seven feet high, fastened at the knee and ankle, on which they stalk, alarmingly masked and clad, waving their arms and gyrating their bodies in a terrifying manner. Long practice, conducted in secret, is needed for the perfecting of the dance, and the young men admitted to the cult are particularly vulnerable during training to the malevolence of their enemies. Evil thoughts directed against them at this time can cause them to fall from the stilts and break their bones, a danger against which they protect themselves by secret tattoo marks and by rubbing various pigments on their bodies. The performance is part of the annual circumcision ceremonies, and its original function was to try the courage of the newly circumcised boys when they emerged from the hut in which they had been immured for two months during the healing process. They were met, presumably at dusk, by these spectral creatures striding through the bush, raising their arms aloft like praying mantises and jingling strings of bells wound round their bodies. They are an unnerving spectacle even now, in broad daylight, for the stilts are clothed in long trousers and the men's faces hidden under scarlet devil-masks, fringed with black hair and whiskers; it would take a stout nerve to face them if one had been told, as the circumcised boys traditionally were, that they were spirits of the dead risen from the grave to meet them. After the first fright the boys were comfortably laughed at and reassured, and the tall spirits, now all identified as neighbouring young men, fell on one another in a mock wrestling match, accompanied by a deafening uproar of jingling and drumming. No doubt it all ended happily with drinking and festivity, but it must have been a daunting introduction to manhood.

Nowadays the youths are no longer subjected to this ordeal, but the dance survives as part of the festivities, attended by eager crowds of men and boys. I went chaperoned by John Ambrose, the young African District Commissioner at Newala, and the *liwali* or elected headman of Mahuta, who shrieked their explanations into my ear through the uproarious din. The performers took an unconscionable time to prepare themselves for the ceremony, and made menacing rushes at us as they passed through the crowd; but it was all done with great good humour and laughter, and the local minstrel, evidently a wag, established himself and his instrument on the bonnet of the Land Rover and could only with difficulty be dislodged for the return journey.

Ionides, when I got home and opened the creaking door from the veranda, seemed not to have stirred; he was still sitting in the gloom where I had left him after breakfast, his feet on the writing-table among his letters, smoking as usual and gazing into space. (I had once asked him, out of curiosity, why there was always so much sand and grit on this table, and he had replied with some surprise, as though noticing the phenomenon for the first time, 'I suppose it comes off my shoes'; an apparent *non sequitur* which was really the only possible explanation.) He listened to my account of the dancing with marked reserve, and I could see that he did not greatly care to hear about it. If it had been a mating display of lizards he would have sat up at once, but human beings have none of the charm of reptiles. He seemed even a little put out that I had absented myself for a whole morning; one moreover which had not been without incident, for in the bushes behind the house he had caught a pair of one-horned giant chameleons. These little primeval dragons were now clambering balefully about their respective boxes, twanging the wire with long claws and turning their leathery eyes in all directions. They had been daffodil-yellow and green when taken, but now had had time to appreciate their situation, and had turned dark grey with displeasure. When I approached the cages they trained a swivelling eye on me, as on a target, and slowly opened their mouths in a raucous hiss. If I had been here, Ionides said, I could have caught them myself; their bite, though sharp, was harmless, and I would have been able to observe the mysterious process by which they turned black when angry, 'Rather like,' he reflectively added, 'some military types.' Now there was nothing for me to do but to eat my tomatoes and onions alone (the midday portion of goat having already been swallowed and being now in the early stages of digestion), while he listened to my account of the dancing and the little I had been able to learn about circumcision ceremonies.

'I don't believe one can help the young; not much,' he said after a pause, drinking his coffee and watching the smoke drifting up from stained fingers. (We had gradually arrived at the subject of youth in general.) 'What's born in a child will come out. If there's nothing there, no amount of teaching and psychology will do him any good.' He is interested, in a detached way, in children, and one of the few regrets that he admits when he considers his solitary life is that he has never had any. He would have liked a couple of good sons, sons with guts; but if they had not been born with guts (a word he is fond of) he is unwilling to suppose that any amount of teaching or example could have helped them. This is a favourite theme, and when I made some mild protest to the effect that children who had a bad start in life and were never helped usually turned out badly, his eyes lit up with a gleam which I later came to associate with ancient history, from which he now drew reinforcements to prove his thesis.

'Well, I don't know: there must be plenty of people who had a disastrous start, yet left their mark on history. Francisco Pizzaro, for example; a nameless bastard brought up *literally* in a pig-sty, eating pig's food. He eventually became the conqueror of Peru, you remember, the man who produced more riches for the Spanish Empire than anyone else. When he was murdered in 1541 he was the supreme ruler of Peru, by far the richest colony in the world.' History is Ionides' favourite reading; he has read widely and forgotten nothing; and when once embarked on the drawing of analogies holds his paralysed listener with a glittering eye, an eye which, cast raptly upward after an elusive thought, gleams with the exaggerated lustre that one sees in the eyes of transfigured saints in the paintings of El Greco. He more closely resembles El Greco's St. Peter than any living person I can call to mind; but the resemblance goes no further than the bony structure. The eye comes down at length, watering from the chase, and the argument is pursued with a glee which could only pejoratively be described as holy.

'Another example that comes to mind is Chaka, surely, the great king of the Zulus, who was driven into exile by his father and ended up as the founder of the Zulu Empire? By the time he was murdered in 1828 he had conquered all the neighbouring tribes in the area. Then what about Mohammed Ahmed, the son of a Dongola boat-maker who became the supreme religious ruler of the Sudan?'

'You mean the Mahdi?'

'The Mahdi, yes. When he died of typhus in 1885 he

was extremely powerful and worshipped by the Sudanese; a man whose name, you'll admit, rings through history. Then again, there was Basil, who ended up, you remember, Emperor of Byzantium. He was merely a stable-boy, who because of his good looks became the favourite of the degenerate emperor of the period.'

'An advantage that you don't put down to his strength of character, surely?'

'Not exactly his strength of character, no, not entirely, but the Emperor happened to be homosexual and in the end Basil murdered him and became emperor himself; a very good emperor too.'

'An improving story.'

'I'm not trying to tell you improving stories, but to prove my point. If you prefer to consider the gentler sex, there's the Empress Wu in the seventh century, who was originally a concubine—just a perfectly ordinary concubine to the Chinese Emperor—who became one of the greatest empresses ever known, a most ruthless woman who ruled with a rod of iron. She had her Gestapo and her torture chambers and all the correct paraphernalia of a dictator, and lived to a ripe old age of over eighty.'

By this time the prevailing style of Ionides' heroes in history was becoming apparent, and the expression 'making good' more clearly defined. He was warming to the work, and we were off on one of those extraordinary monologues which commonly started at seven o'clock, at breakfast, and went on until snake-news brought relief, or until I was exhausted.

'Then what about the great Minister of Police in France in the Napoleonic period, Josef Fouché? He started as the son of a poor Nantes fisherman, became a small seminary teacher, and ended up as Duke of Otranto, a multi-millionaire and Minister of Police. Before he got exiled, of course; he overstepped the mark a bit with the Emperor, but he was a multi-millionaire to the end. And his great enemy Talleyrand—though it's true *he* was an aristocrat;

he was Duke of Périgord and Bishop of Autun; but at that period the sons of aristocrats were just left to be dragged up by the grooms. . . .' He reflected briefly, casting up his eyes. 'He must, I suppose, have had *some* education because he was Bishop of Autun at a very early age, but in his childhood, I think, he had no care or attention at all. My authority for that, by the way, is Duff Cooper's book. Then there were those very remarkable people who sprang up at the time of the revolution of the slaves of San Domingo. Jean Jacques Dessalines was a slave of the most violent and ignorant type, but wouldn't you say that he became a most brilliant general?'

Defeated already but guessing that there was more to come, I inquired faintly about the date.

'He was murdered by his own people in 1806. He was the one who finally completed the liberation of San Domingo in 1803. But the greatest of them all, of course, was Toussaint—though he *did* have some education, in spite of being born a slave and the son of a slave. Christophe, the king who took over when Dessalines was murdered, only learned to write his name towards the end of his life; a very progressive king, too, but in the end he became tyrannical; his people turned against him, he got a sort of partial paralysis and shot himself with a golden bullet in 1820. And we mustn't forget Tippu Tib, to *my* mind the greatest of all the African explorers, half-Arab, half-Swahili, belonging to quite a small family and in any case a half-caste. He became the ruler of the greater part of the Congo; it was through him that Stanley was able to do his explorations, and play the part he did in the scramble for Africa. Tippu Tib died in 1905 a very rich and generous man, helping everyone in Zanzibar, a most respected figure.'

'Wasn't he also a great slaver?'

'The slaving was incidental, just one of the departments. He was primarily a trader. And I'm sure you remember Henry Morgan the pirate, a man of no origins who ended up as deputy governor of Jamaica; a very remarkable man, though perhaps not a wholly likeable one; perhaps, in certain ways, not of the very highest ethics. . . .'

The list grows longer and longer, without any sign of flagging or slowing down. Henry Morgan the pirate is followed by Barbarossa and other Barbary corsairs, by L'Ollonais, who first put piracy on a paying basis and did very well before he was caught and tortured to death by an Indian from Darien, until finally we arrive, as we usually do, at the early Mongols, and the great name of Genghis Khan is brought out, as it almost invariably is, to clinch the argument. Genghis too, it seems, had a bad start, was driven out into the snow where he scavenged for food like an animal and trained himself for the struggle for power in which, as I was now in no danger of forgetting, he was so splendidly successful.

Ionides' heroes all have a streak of violence in their nature, as he has himself; they are men of action, conquerors, robbers and military geniuses; some of them he learned to admire while he was still at school and discovered the campaigns of Joshua and Sennacherib in the Bible, the military prodigies of Hannibal in the pages of Livy. He has never cared much for Napoleon and only grudgingly admires him, 'a small, mean man, something unlikeable about him'; his favourites are all those who show an antique fierceness, facing death with indifference when they have no other weapon. 'Jezebel now, I always liked her; a great woman, who died so bravely, with such dignity.' It is the same feeling that he has for all wild animals, and especially for snakes; a good animal, a good snake is the one with courage to defend itself, to give him a run for his money at close quarters and threaten him with death on equal terms. There is no reptile, however modest, to which he is indifferent, but the ones that enthral him are always those that carry the lure of danger—the beautiful *thanatophidia*, the death snakes. Even in reading Shakespeare, which he constantly does, keeping a tattered omnibus volume on the floor beside him, it is the references to animals that he pauses over and can copiously quote, knowing most of them by heart. 'I like *Venus and Adonis*, don't you? That description of the wild boar, digging graves with his tusks, the bristles on his back, and so on. . . .

' "On his bow-back he hath a battle set
Of bristly pikes, that ever threat his foes;
His eyes like glow-worms shine when he doth fret;
His snout digs sepulchres where'er he goes;
  Being moved, he strikes whate'er is in his way,
  And whom he strikes his crooked tushes slay."

Oh, good stuff.' It is an accurate description, for one thing, and he likes the boar as much as he likes the poetry; his eyes light up with a gleam of genuine sympathy.

III

GABOON VIPERS AND GREEN MAMBAS

BY the time the rising sun had scaled the roof and touched the tops of the palms below the veranda, the gaboon vipers which had been lazily prowling the thicket during the night hours would all have vanished, concealed under drifts of brushwood and dead leaves. They are nocturnal snakes and marvellously lethargic; even their hunting is done with a minimum of exertion, lying concealed and motionless until a rat, a bird or some other luckless vermin comes their way, and then, as Ionides says, only if they are really hungry taking a crack at it. They feed at intervals of about six weeks, live at a mysteriously slow tempo, and pass the greater part of their lives in sleep. The amount of venom they secrete is extravagantly in excess of anything they might need for killing their prey; this, and their *trompe l'oeil* camouflage, is their defence, and being so copious and deadly it is a little surprising that they use it so rarely, appearing to be always taken unawares whenever they are caught. The explanation apparently is that the nature of the country they inhabit has been altered by man in the course of the last few decades, too short a time for even the slightest evolutionary adaptation. Perhaps fifty years ago the Makonde plateau and plain were clothed with primal forest; these snakes were rarely seen and had few enemies—their only enemy is man and in those days he was scarcer—and their protective suit, painted in a bold geometric design of ochre, brown and black, was all they needed to keep them safe from harm. The forest hid them from cruising kites and eagles, and if a man chanced to come their way, in the gloom of the leaves it was almost impossible to see them. Now the nature of the country is drastically altered: the forest trees have all been felled or burned, to be succeeded by a secondary growth of scrub thicket, through which a vastly increased human population scratches the earth and maintains a rotation of crops which, haphazard and dense enough to the casual eye, affords a very inferior protection. But these large and powerful snakes, faithful to instincts that have served for a million years, have observed no change; like the Egyptian Copts, whom Browne, the eighteenth-century traveller, saw 'settled in the composure of ignorance', they lie wrapped in a dream of security in village rubbish-heaps, under drifts of leaves where women search daily for firewood, in the dead grass at the side of well-worn paths. The mystery is that they have not long ago been exterminated; before Ionides came to live in the area they were killed and eaten whenever they were seen, being full of meat, and he himself has captured over a thousand. Yet there seems to be no diminution of their numbers, which is puzzling; the fact delights him though he cannot account for it; and certainly on many of the days when we went out together he added eight or nine and occasionally more to the caged and coiled contingent in the living-room.

The day after my arrival news came early; the Land Rover was crammed with men and gear and we set off from the house a little before nine o'clock. The speed of our departure, then as on every succeeding day, was extraordinary; Rashidi murmured a word in the doorway and Ionides sprang to life and disappeared with such suddenness that I was left struggling to my feet and falling over myself, as though we had been surprised by a fire alarm. The moment I was aboard we started with a jerk and drove for several dusty miles in silence; after the morning hours of indolence and talk the atmosphere had changed to one of concentration, almost of suspense, Ionides staring ahead with the single-minded stillness of a pointer.

We turned off the road presently on to a bush path, where thorny branches began to claw at the vehicle. Ionides shut the window smartly and lit another cigarette. We bumped and ground our way across several shambas, untidy patches of cassava and pockets of swaying millet which I was only just beginning to distinguish from the bush, and came to a stop in a small clearing among native huts, where an expectant group was already waiting for us. The daily snake-catching stands high in the local catalogue of entertainments; life in the bush is a placid affair in which very little happens, and the eruption of the Land Rover scattering chickens in a village, or better still the sight of Ionides himself striding purposefully at the head of a cavalcade carrying snake-sticks and boxes, is always the signal for a crowd to gather, for men and boys to come whooping and running in his wake, even for women to snatch up their babies and come circling softly round the edge of the excitement, uttering little squeals and clucks of comment. Ionides disregards the audience, but I suspect enjoys it; it is a good one, avid for the drama, willing to scream and run on the smallest excuse, enthralled by the payment which follows successful capture. He makes no concessions in return, affecting to regard them as a great nuisance and muttering fiercely when they come too close; but I more than once saw a gleam in his eye and observed him walk away with the innocent off-hand air of one who knows he has given a good performance.

On this first occasion as on many others, the snake was so well concealed that it was difficult to imagine how anyone could possibly know that it was there. All one could see was a pile of twigs and leaves, but there was a youth beside it who rose from a squatting position and pointed impassively down at the tangled heap. Ionides inspected the position briefly for signs of interference ('jiggery-pokery') and began gently to lift the leaves with a metal-tipped stick. The interior of the mass looked the same, all leaves and compost, but he quickly handed the stick to Rashidi and squatted on his hams, though I could still see nothing. He groped beside him for a pair of tongs, and screwing up his eyes against the cigarette smoke (he was still smoking) extended his hand and gently touched a leaf in the centre of the nest. And then I saw it, for the leaf flinched, and was not a leaf at all but the creature's head, and the whole centre of the hollow, dusty and brown and black like all the rest, suddenly revealed itself as the richly sober coils of a large snake.

He now changed his position from the collapsed squat into which he falls so easily, and casting the tongs aside, knelt with some care at the edge of the heap, pausing only to shift the cigarette from his mouth to the fingers of one hand. He rocked on his knees, finding a firm balance, and to the sound of breathing from the onlookers hovered for a moment over the body before swooping to a powerful grip at the back of the neck. The movement was so quick that neither I nor the snake had been prepared for it; the next instant he was crouching back on his heels with the head held well away from him and his left hand firmly grasping the arched body, which one now saw was about four feet long, compact with powerful muscle and as bright as a tapestry. The head, a moment before so artfully concealed, revealed itself as thick and spade-shaped, with steady topaz eyes underlined and emphasized with a cunning cosmetic stroke. The face had a curiously mild and dog-like look, and the tongue, when he eased his grip and it flickered from the neat little hole at the point of the muzzle, was moist and brilliant, a tendril of pink and black.

The onlookers fell back with chirping cries and the women scampered away to greater safety. He made no attempt to display it, but carried it ceremoniously forward and dropped it with a ritual movement into the box. The gesture was grave yet brisk, and I was struck then, as on many later occasions, by a sort of priestly rhythm in his proceedings, as though daily repetition had staled nothing but had added the grace of discipline to the mystery. This fancy, once embarked on, could be infinitely extended; the aura of authority surrounding him, the stern demeanour, the initiate's proud jealousy of his office, even the austerity and celibate solitude of his life all contribute to a recurring image of conscious priesthood, at which he would certainly scoff, but which is none the less valid. The Africans who congregate daily for the snake ceremony share, I am almost sure, this hazy impression; they may squeal and scamper, crowd round the box to peer, elbowing one another as though at a freak-show; but beneath their capers is always a touch of awe; the prevailing mood of the thing is esoteric.

Money was handed over in a respectful silence, and while the box was lifted on to a close-cropped head, Ionides squatted once more on his heels to enter the details of the catch in his little book. Species, sex, place, time of day, money paid out, the tribe of the recipient are all written down in ink with leisurely precision. Not until the record was complete did he rise to his feet, hand over the pen and book without a glance and set off along the track leading back to the vehicle.

On the way to the next snake I pursued him with questions; it seemed so strange that this dangerous creature, so well equipped with venom and strength, should have offered so little resistance. 'Yes, well; it depends what you mean by dangerous. I dare say if I had sufficiently provoked the animal, if I had *asked* it to bite me, it probably would; but it's a good-tempered snake; as you saw, remarkably placid. They're nocturnal, as you know. At this hour of the day they're soundly asleep, or at least drowsy. You saw how I touched this one on the top of the head; that's to find out whether it's torpid or partly alert; in this case, you remember, there was a slight shiver, but it didn't attempt to move. They've relied on their natural protection for millions of years, and you can't expect them to revolutionize their habits. In the first place, they don't expect to be seen, and if they *are* uncovered they rely on their camouflage and immobility. I don't know how quickly you saw that the snake was there, but it takes a bit of practice. Then, if none of these devices works and the snake's disturbed, it has two others up its sleeve which are very useful. It can intimidate, swelling its body up like an inflated tyre—all the vipers can do that—and letting off a menacing hiss which is pretty efficacious. And if that doesn't persuade you to let it alone of course it can kill you with its bite. Death from a gaboon viper is singularly unpleasant; the venom's haemotoxic and neurotoxic—haemorrhages, constricted breathing, bleeding from all the orifices of the body and from old scars, oh very thorough—but I naturally avoid giving it the chance to bite, and I must say, to do it justice, that it very rarely does, even when it has the most enviable opportunities. They're immensely plentiful in this area; I've caught over a thousand, but I've never heard of anyone being bitten. I've often stroked them with my hand before catching them, and I really believe, I'm *almost* sure though I haven't tried it, that you could actually tread on one with your naked foot, and if you didn't hurt it, it wouldn't do more than hiss and try to get away. It's a most obliging snake; unlike the mambas it seems relatively indifferent to captivity. You'll see when we get home, if I catch any more, how amiably they all settle down together. The thing I can't account for is why there are so many left, for these people used to kill them and eat them in thousands before I put a stop to it, and I've done my share in reducing the population. Yet they even seem, round here, to be increasing.'

He is apt to speak in this off-hand way about snake-bite, but the off-handedness is only apparent; in practice he is immensely careful, and fiercely impatient of people who take risks. Serum and hypodermic needles are always carried in the Land Rover, though he has never yet used them on himself, in spite of having been bitten nine times; he carries them on the supposition that sooner or later somebody else may get bitten, or he himself get a bite which could be serious. 'If I got a *full* bite from a mamba or gaboon viper, even now, I should use it at once.' But I wonder whether, in the event of such an accident to himself, he would really use it, for he has a dread of old age and considers death completely unimportant. 'From the time I first started living this kind of life I've always assumed the probability of a violent death, and it still seems to me the natural and sensible one.' It is not, to be precise, the thought of old age that he abhors, since he considers himself to have reached that stage already; it is decrepitude, and he admits that he gambles on 'one of these things getting me, before *that* happens'—a safe gamble, he thinks, on the law of averages. He considers that by now he has developed a fair immunity to snake venom, and that a bite which might kill another man would probably not be fatal in his case.

Most of the bites he has had have been only partial, a graze from a boomslang, a puncture from one fang of a puff-adder, a deep bite from another which had already struck several times and missed, and so partly exhausted its venom. He has deliberately caused a snake to bite him on four occasions out of curiosity, to test the efficacy of an antidote recommended by a witch-doctor of his acquaintance. The effect was no more than pain and swelling and a temporary paralysis, but he cannot accept the experiment as conclusive since herbal concoctions injected under the skin have never been found to have any effect on venom, and by that time he had probably achieved, through accidental bites, a measure of immunity. It is not from bravado but for the sake of this immunity, which he is anxious to increase, that he has refrained from using serum after being bitten, taking notes of his reactions, the degree of pain and swelling and other symptoms, anxiously weighing each stage in the fine balance between danger and recovery. He is annoyed by the stories acquaintances sometimes tell of his melodramatic carelessness with snakes—mambas loose on the living-room floor, a boomslang slung over his shoulder like a bandolier, a puff-adder coiling about on the breakfast table. He is never careless. 'People usually prefer a sensational lie to the truth, in my experience. Wouldn't you agree? You must have heard or read those stories people still relentlessly tell about Africa, when they think they can't be checked up on. Elephants besieging people in caves, lionesses wrecking aeroplanes, spitting-cobras attacking Land Rovers and savaging the occupants. There's even one, rather widely circulated, about my letting a black mamba crawl over my lap in the lavatory. And—though you may not believe this—that old chestnut about the mamba killing nine people in a hut (a hardy perennial whenever people start telling tall stories about snakes), has actually got into print as happening to *me*. Proper emetics.'

The taking of gaboon vipers went on day after day with great regularity, until one almost lost the sense of its being dramatic. Occasionally the snake would stir and show annoyance, swelling up its heavy body with an appearance of anger and giving a prolonged hiss as it deflated, but only one that I saw made any serious attempt to get away, pouring its length majestically over the leaves, the ribs rowing rhythmically under the patterned skin as it moved ponderously off in search of cover. But the mambas were very different. They were alert, sharp-sighted and supernaturally agile, melting away before one's eyes in the brilliant green and sun-dazzle of the leaves, to re-appear magically in another inaccessible outpost of the tree, swan-neck raised above emerald coils, elegant head turned intently after the pursuer, whom they follow with the rapt gaze of a cunning bird. They love the brilliant foliage of the huge mango trees, which in sunlight exactly matches their own green, and lie all day in the warmth of the top-most branches, swaying in the wind, coiled like a silken rope and almost invisible. But Africans have sharp eyes, and spend much of their life sitting about in the sun with nothing to do, so that sooner or later a fluttering and scolding bird will catch their attention, a bending twig or a polished coil will be noticed, and a watch be set on the little coronet above, swaying in apparent security in its high nest.

I found them at first impossible, and always extremely difficult to see; looking up from the base of the tree, in its spreading shade, was like peering for some distant detail of mosaic in the dark roof of a cathedral. Mango trees have silvery limbs, bare as columns, reaching up into the gloom of foliage like a supporting structure, and the vault o leaves, arched and densely dark as a great dome, is pierced by sequins of sunlight which move and dazzle. Ionides and the two boys, Rashidi and Pétu, would sometimes stand for a long time looking upwards, plotting a course which would bring them close to the snake. They are always quiet, so as not to disturb it (snakes are deaf but wonderfully sensitive to vibration), and after a while, conferring in whispers and pointing, one of the boys will clasp the trunk and begin cautiously to climb. In the old days Ionides used to go up the trees himself, but his lameness prevents him now and he is not sorry; he has a poor head for heights. Instead he waits at the bottom with his grab-stick, head thrown back, shading his eyes with his hand; his sharpness of vision is as good as ever, and he gives occasional directions to the climber, who by this time may be lost in a maze of leaves.

At the first mamba-catching I saw there were two snakes, coiled together in the topmost plateau of leaves perhaps fifty feet from the ground, and there was a ripple of laughter when a black arm was thrown up to point and a woman cried out gleefully that they were making love. Certainly they seemed unaware of danger; their coils were wreathed together like a garland, and the leaves moved slightly in a way that was different from the gentle stir of the breeze. Rashidi, the senior snake-hand, who climbs (or so it seemed to me) only when there is a particularly good audience, murmured something to Pétu, who sought about on the bole of the tree for a grip, and with the serious and modest air which never leaves him began methodically to climb. He went always barefoot in the early days of my visit (for a reason which had nothing to do with climbing and which I was to discover later) and his black legs and feet went steadily up the smooth limbs until he had reached a point of rest where he could pause and look down, stretching out his hand for the top of the long grab being softly passed up to him. This is a hollow metal tube fifteen feet along, with hinged claws at the top which are opened and closed by a lever at the lower end, and which can be locked by a screw. It is not unlike a pruning implement, except that the cusps, instead of meeting together like scissors on a cutting edge, are smooth, and close on the body of the snake more like a handcuff on a wrist, uncomfortably tight, perhaps, but hardly painful.

He now climbed further out of sight, trailing the grab after him and searching for a secure fork into which he could wedge his body, and for a branch on which the heavy pole could be rested while he passed it cautiously up in the right direction. The snakes seemed still unconscious, and sinec Pétu had now climbed so high as to be almost invisible except for the pallid blur of his ragged shorts, I came out into the sun and stood at a little distance, from which I could detect the ring of green which was not leaves, swaying with halcyon calm in its lofty cradle. Suddenly there was a glint of metal as the jaws of the grab closed over a looped coil, and a whip-lash of green flung out from the top of the tree, the long body casting and coiling, but held fast. A small head appeared momentarily out of the leaves, turning on a slender neck to take stock of the thing that so inexplicably held it, and then withdrew abruptly into the foliage, which rippled with its tentative efforts to follow its mate. But the metal jaws, which had caught it a little behind the middle of the body, held fast and were not to be eluded, and it tried first one direction and then another, gliding off at speed among the leaves and curving back in dismay a moment after, staring in fierce astonishment at the trap.

Ionides and Rashidi were now beside me, holding up their grabs like lances in the air, waiting for the moment when Pétu could lower the snake within their reach. It was difficult to disentangle from the tree, coiling its long tail among the branches, winding like a tendril round handfuls of leaves and twigs, desperately seeking a hold, a balance, any purchase which might give leverage and set it free. But it was thrust out at last, and appeared suddenly against the sky, looping and winding about the pole like the caduceus of the ancients, the rod of Hermes, and was tilted slowly outwards and finally down. The waiting grabs were ready with open jaws; as soon as the snake was within reach they closed upon it, a careful distance apart; the metal grab was released on a word of command and the living knot, like a trophy proudly borne on the points of spears, came down to be laid at length on the dusty ground.

Here at last the beautiful creature could be seen at close quarters, no longer freely moving with an effortless ripple, threading like a ribbon of green through the spangled tree, but humbled by the metal cuffs locked on its body, writhing in the grip of an enemy it would never comprehend. But it was not defeated. It reared up as far as it could and struck at the trap, attacking the hard metal with smooth jaws, so that venom ran down and trickled in drops on the sand. When Ionides approached it turned and faced him, its smooth green head, so curiously, with its full dark eye, like the head of a bird, and measured the distance, waiting for the unknown enemy to come within range. He crouched before it, slowly advancing the tongs as though hypnotised, the gaze of man and snake intent on the point at which one would suddenly dart and the other evade, both warily watching and measuring, avid for the strike. The tongs struck first, and missed; like a flash the head had eluded the thrust and was poised afresh, neck arched and eyes unwavering; a thread of tongue flickered nervously in and out. Ionides moved closer and struck again, and this time the snake was caught at the end of the tongs, its bright head flattened and distorted under pressure, the eyes covered, the forked tongue protruding, grains of sand and dirt dribbling from the lips. No further movement was possible; the body was trapped in two places and the head compressed; only the end of the tail, the few inches not wrapped tightly around the shafts, continued to flail about for a fresh hold, whipping little marks and grooves in the soft dust.

Ionides held the tongs in one hand and groped behind him with the other. Rashidi was ready with a calico bag which he put over it like a glove, and the muffled hand came forward to take a careful grip round the neck of the snake. The tongs were discarded, and the snake's head, which a moment before I had thought irretrievably damaged, at once resumed its bird-like shape; the tongue flickered, the delicate pale jaws were slightly open, and the eyes, dark and intent as ever, still kept their unblinking watch on the chance of escape. I had been wrong in supposing that the head had suffered; the bones of the skull are supple, the skin elastic, and Ionides knows to a nicety what pressure to exert. He is concerned only to control the head and keep the mouth closed while he gets his hand on the neck in a safe grip; once that is achieved the snake is powerless to bite, and need never feel the grabs or tongs again. Before the holds are released, however, the snake must be sexed, and while the head is held firmly by hand the grabs are kept locked, and an assistant must grasp the thrashing tail and turn the vent upwards, massaging vigorously with a thumb until the sexual organs, powerless even in this humiliating posture to resist the stimulus of friction, moistly emerge from a neat aperture and reveal the sex of the captive for the written record.

Having watched Rashidi and Pétu a number of times I was soon allowed to perform this office myself, and had my first experience of handling a wild snake. The feeling is quite unlike one's expectation, the first touch conveying surprised pleasure, since the body is smooth and warm and urgently alive, so that contact with one's palm is reassuring, a pleasurable shock like physical recognition. But the snake is not reassured, and the little vent, held tight in its ring of protective muscle, withholds its secret; at first my thumb was too timid and considerate and the whip-like tail wound tightly around my wrist in a grip of protest. 'Harder,' said Ionides, 'rub harder,' and I indelicately pressed and urged with a circular motion until the lips of the aperture relaxed and a bud-like structure appeared and then another, as though one had been squeezing the secret organs of a plant. At the same time a bright orange fluid sprayed out and ran over my hand, vivid and granular, like liquid pollen, and Ionides was pointing to two little jutting protruberances, slanting stiffly away from each other in a sideways direction, and asking if I could see the two penises. I had not known that there would be two, and relaxed my pressure in surprise, upon which the curious manifestation vanished like magic, the vent contracted, and the smooth underbody of the snake was as neat, as polished, as secretive as before. 'I'm sorry it's defecated on your hand,' said Ionides in a matter-of-fact voice, 'but don't relax your grip. You've got to roll the body up and get it in the bag.' (The pollen-coloured fluid, I afterwards found, had a faintly spicy smell like curry powder, perfectly inoffensive.)

The grabs were unlocked and the writhing coils were free to move against me; to my unpractised hands it was not as easy as it looked. Rashidi had always done it with as brisk an unconcern as though he had been coiling rope, but a seven-foot mamba can make many loops and knots which slide between finger and thumb and are alive with a thousand glissades for eluding capture, and as fast as I had it coiled in a knot it would break out into arabesques and cunning scrolls, so that I looked with despair from the snake to the bag, and wondered how I should ever get them together.

But if the onlookers were amused, Ionides was immovable and patient, squatting with left arm hidden in the bag and the bright head of the snake held fast through the cloth; and at last the writhing coils were under control and held in my one hand as close to the head as I dared, while with the other I drew the mouth of the bag down his arm and thrust the tangle of mamba into the interior. Now, having let go, I had to draw up the tape of the bag to close it, and at this I was clumsy, while the snake was not; if it had spent its life, an arboreal Houdini, practising the strategy of this escape it could not have been more skilful; loop after loop rose up from the interior to the mouth, forcing the tape apart, pouring out in a smooth lassoo over my hands, running out its tendril of tail across my knees and whipping about for a purchase on my clothing. But at last it was secure and the bag closed, and I had only to knot the tape in the proper manner. This was always done by winding the tape twice round the neck of the bag and once round one's left thumb, to make a convenient loop through which the end could be finally pulled fast; but in my anxiety I bound in my thumb so tightly that it could not be freed, and there was another delay, much enjoyed by the spectators, who, now that the snake was out of sight, pressed so enthusiastically close that I could hardly see what I was doing and could feel their knees against the small of my back, while the snake lunged this way and that inside the calico and it looked as though we were permanently shackled together. A timely snarl from Ionides, however, caused them to fall back; my thumb was extricated and the end of the tape thrust through the loop and pulled as tight as my inexperience would allow. Even this was not enough, and Rashidi improved the knot before Ionides would let go.

Then I was told to get out of the way and scrambled to my feet while the bag was tossed lightly into the shallow box which all this time had been waiting to receive it. The snake surged blindly about in the bag for a moment or two, rearing its head and striking at random; a little patch of venom appeared and spread like a teardrop through the fabric. Now it was time to close the box, and Ionides took the tongs and gently pressed the moving bag into place while the lid, swivelling loosely from a nail, was manœuvred into position and hammered down. We should none of us see that mamba again, even at the Sunday ceremony of packing, for these beautiful snakes are too active and dangerous for handling; once caught and confined they are left to grow calm and comatose in their bags, which they quickly do, emerging only in the snake-pit or reptile house at the end of their journey. This handsome male had reached the end of his life as a wild creature, and before the last nail had been driven home Ionides was already searching for his mate. She had moved fast, and had already arrived at the other side of the tree, at the tip of a great branch which overhung some smaller scrub in the thicket. A dozen hands pointed to where she was, herself like a leafless branch swaying out from the foliage, her eyes on the next tree, measuring the distance, making her magical rope-bridge through the air while her long tail slid and coiled through the twigs of the mango. In this perilous manœuvre she was a perfect target, and from below the grabs rose eagerly to reach her. In the same moment, half-way across and supported only by her own strength, she saw them coming, and turned back in mid-air in a magnificent unhurried loop which was drawn at once into cover of the foliage. But it was too late; Pétu was already high in the tree with the long grab; there was a sharp click, the branch shuddered, and with a tearing of leaves she was lowered into the shade where two pairs of open jaws were waiting to receive her.

I never became wholly reconciled to the moment of

capture, to seeing the bright creature, which a moment before was as much a part of the tree as the glossy leaves, brought to the ground and humbled in hateful manacles. All traps are hateful, and the pinch of those metal claws, so efficient and mechanical in their grip that the utmost effort of flesh could make no impression, had something monstrous about it. Ionides, I believe, shares to some degree this feeling of abhorrence, though we never discussed it; there was always a moment of relief between us when the screws were released and the living snake was held in our bare hands. He has, indeed, a dislike of all mechanical contrivances, which he despises; if it were possible to take these snakes from their trees without their aid, with only forked sticks and nooses, as in his early days, he would greatly prefer it. But of course it is not. They are too well equipped for flight and defence, too miraculously agile and alert, only too well able to deal death and disappear through their territory of leaves, where man climbs only slowly and laboriously. In the high trees which are their province, if it were not for the cunning of grabs, they would be safe for ever; a creature that lives by hunting birds, and can surprise them with sudden death as they alight from the air, is more than a match for any man, no matter how stealthy a climber. So Ionides uses his tools, and has as much respect for them as he is able to feel for anything not alive; but the pleasure of capture is diminished by their use, and the moment it is possible to do so he discards them.

It must, I suppose, be rare to see a mamba catching a bird, though village Africans, sitting vacantly in the shade through such interminable hours, their eyes fixed on nothing until a leaf stirs or a beetle makes a foray in the dust, must sometimes have the luck to see it happen. I saw it once, as clearly as though the act were performed for my benefit, and it was so surely done, in such a minimal fraction of time, that it was finished and over before my senses accepted it. We had had news of a large snake in a mango tree; the place was nowhere near a village and for once we were free of the usual noisy convoy and came silently up the sandy track through high millet, making no disturbance. The tree stood in a little clearing, and after standing still for a while, shading our eyes, we saw the snake quite clearly, coiled in the sun on a swaying cradle of leaves. As we looked, a bird flew blithely across from another tree and alighted with spread wings; or almost alighted; for the snake seemed to strike while it was yet in the air, and the bird disappeared in the leaves in a sharp flurry. Nothing more happened, and having carefully taken his bearings Pétu advanced to the tree and began to climb. Stealthy though he was, some tremor of his approach must have reached the snake, for before he was half-way up its visible coils became invisible and something fell with a tiny thud at my feet. It was the bird, an African starling, its plumage unruffled, its eyes open, its body still pliant and warm with the movement of life. But it was quite dead, without any visible mark; the snake had dropped it in fright, and now it would be wasted.

I took it in my hand and squatted under the tree to examine it at leisure. The plumage was blue-green and glossy, the breast the colour of red earth and marvellously soft. It looked so perfect and alive that at first I supposed it to be only stunned, and stroked the breast and back with the tip of a finger, even breathing into my cupped hands in the futile belief that it would presently stir. But we waited a long time under that mango tree while Pétu hunted the mamba, which was now well aware of him and leading a mazy dance from branch to branch; and presently the delicate claws began to close, the eyes became less bright, and the head fell limply over the edge of my hand. The warm and perfect body was full of poison, of a secretion so venomous that the merest fraction of a drop would have been enough to put so weightless a creature to death; and long before the snake was brought down the warmth in my hand was fading, and the beauty had mysteriously gone from the thing I was holding, so that I put it down at last without regret.

Only one of all the mambas that I saw caught came to grief in the catching, and this was one which was hiding in a thorn thicket, where it was hard to see and the grabs difficult to operate. These secondary-growth trees are dense and unpleasant; they grow together in impenetrable masses and strong-stemmed climbing plants weave all over their foliage like a net. It is easy for the snake to hide and resist capture; unseen in a mesh of stems and leaves there are a thousand twigs round which it can wind its body, and the thorns impede the grabs and make climbing impossible. In this case it was thorns and not the grabs which did the damage; at one moment the snake reared up from the foliage, taking her bearings, and the waiting grab closed cleanly round her, gripping her tightly a little behind the head. Rashidi pulled, but she had lashed herself to the branches, and there was a cautious tug-of-war, the mamba's body stretched from the tree like a rope, resolutely coming no further. Leaves tore, twigs cracked and broke, but still the snake held fast, and the distressful backward turning of the head suggested that this tautness was not due to strength alone, but that she was caught between the grab and some obstruction. At last something gave, and with a grunt of effort Rashidi levered her outwards from the tree. But it was not a branch that had broken; she had been held in thorns, and the spines had cut through the skin like a bunch of razors. The green covering remained aloft in the tree, and the snake which dangled at last from the pole was flayed to the tip, gleaming as pink as coral. She came down in a gust of laughter, any physical mishap being irresistible to Africans, and arched and coiled in the dust which stuck to her moist flesh in sordid patterns.

Ionides looked sick, and I turned away. The transformation was too horrible; I had not the stomach to watch her attack the trap with tender jaws, as though even in this plight some desperate hope of escape were still possible.

Ionides called for his knife in a fierce voice; he was holding the head to the ground with a forked stick and was intent on putting an end to the obscene spectacle. When I looked again it was all over; he was gathering the snake, still faintly stirring, into his hands, scowling at the merry on-lookers and elbowing them out of his way with imprecations. He hid the body as deeply as he could under the leaves and thorns, threw down some money on the ground and walked away. It was the only occasion on which ew made the journey home without speaking.

IV

HOME COMPANIONS

IF at first I had thought Ionides' house depressing and his way of life perverse in its discomforts, the mood was transitory. I discovered that by doing without a great many things which most people find necessary he was pursuing a policy towards a definite end. What he wanted, what he had largely got, was freedom. His house was not a home, but a home was something he had never wanted. What he required was a base, a place where he could keep his few possessions and leave when he chose, even at a moment's notice. It is one of his theories that one grows stale if one stays long in one environment (he calls it 'rotting') and when he was younger he had even considered that the longest time it was wholesome to remain anywhere was four days. Even now he lives no more than three months of the year at Newala, moving off into Kenya or Uganda as the fit takes him, ostensibly hunting for snakes but also, I suspect, avoiding the sensation of being settled anywhere, which to his wandering spirit is anathema.

The price to be paid for this unfettered existence is a refusal to submit to what he calls 'the tyranny of possessions'. With few exceptions he dislikes owning things, and it is possible to sit with him in his uninhabited-looking room and at a glance to see nearly everything that he would call his own. His home-made folding table, for which he has no sentimental regard, but keeps because he finds its height convenient; his ugly African-made deck chair, the canvas dark with grease where he rests his head; his snake-catching tools, lying oiled and cleaned and straight against the wall; a portable gramophone which works on batteries, not very satisfactorily, with which he occasionally amuses himself by listening to opera; a heavy wooden box beside his chair, which he never allows anyone to touch, and in which he keeps everything that he considers important. The contents are simple: the ledgers in which he enters his scientific records, his diaries, which contain nothing more personal than his movements from place to place and the snakes he has caught, with their Latin names and sex, and a few volumes on his special subject that he prizes (Charles Pitman's *Snakes of Uganda* is one of his bibles) wedged in with a mixed collection of documents and papers. This box accompanies him on all his journeys and he packs it himself, an eccentricity which has earned it the reputation of concealing some powerful magic. Nothing less, it is argued, could account for his lowering himself to so menial a task, and it is, I am sure, the only one he is ever seen to perform. When the whole household pulls itself up by the roots and takes off for some other country he takes no share in the upheaval beyond saying, in a meaningful voice, 'Let everything necessary be packed', and his rages over any stupidity or negligence are so thoroughly understood that everything, through twenty-four hours of chaotic scuffling and grunting, *is* packed, and he has nothing to do but to walk briskly out to the Land Rover at the moment of departure.

Beyond these few objects he owns nothing, so far as I could discover, but his books and clothing. Those books which are not in the magic box are rarely disturbed; they live in the bedroom book-cases, veiled under dust and cobwebs which would do for a film-set of Miss Havisham's bedroom; and his spare clothes, removed from several small drawers on the day of my arrival, spent the rest of my stay on a chair in the small back-bedroom, which easily accommodated them. I do not think he owns more than one pair of shoes; brown sand-shoes, rather loose, with a little hole in each where the big toe frets them; the laces are never untied, once he has been driven to the extremity of discarding the old and purchasing a new pair; in his view the daily tying and untying of shoe-laces is one of the futile rituals with which modern man is burdened. Socks he disapproves of, and he possesses none, wearing even his evening mosquito boots over bare feet. Socks wrinkle, they go into holes, and must occasionally be washed. When I protested that they saved my ankles from a multitude of scratches he pulled up his trouser from a bare shank and invited me to observe that *his* skin had long ago reached a stage of toughness against which even the thorns of the African bush were powerless. His legs, I thought, bore the traces of old scars, but the meagre covering on the bones was leathery and the sinews hard, so that I was bound to agree that for him socks were probably unnecessary. So much was unnecessary when you came to think of it, that I came to see even the modest contents of my canvas bags as excessive. Little as I had, I could have done with less, and I thought with dismay of the self-indulgent paraphernalia with which I had long been accustomed to travel in Europe.

The prevailing mood, in fact, of our domestic life was very similar to that which romantically affected many people of my parents' generation when they first read Thoreau's *Walden*. This book, I remembered from my childhood, had produced a temporary but violent effect on my mother, who for months had roamed about the house in a highly critical spirit, pouncing on dearly-bought furnishings and ornaments which she felt she could do without. She had been particularly struck by the fact that Thoreau, in his home-made simple-life paradise in the Massachusetts woods, had finally discarded his door-mat as an effete refinement inimical to nature, and had put hers out of sight for a time, though she was too frugal to destroy it. It came back in due course when the fit was over, and she was tired of muddy footprints on the floor; but she never quite lost her hankering for the simple life, though she suffered too from the malady of excessive cleanliness, so that, though my memory brought up this incident of the abandoned door-mat, I could not feel that she would have been happy in Newala.

Most surprising of all, perhaps, for a man who has been so passionate, so obsessive a hunter, is the total absence of trophies. Nothing, of course, is displayed on the walls by way of decoration—such an idea would be entirely foreign to him—but neither is there a horn, a skull, an antler, a claw to be found anywhere, even on a dusty shelf or in a corner; he simply lacks any feeling for accumulation. Not many people in East Africa go in for displaying the heads and horns of big game; the climate and insect pests between them make it impracticable, and most of the trade which supports the taxidermists of Nairobi is done for museums and for the American businessmen who cherish the tangible proof of their costly safaris. (And proof is not always perhaps the right word; trophies are often supplied confidentially, to order, and Ionides has more than once, with cynical pleasure, provided data as to how a particular animal had supposedly been shot.) But most hunters keep something, even if it is only the claws of a man-eating lion or the skull of a leopard, or a particularly fine skin which they cannot bear to part with. Ionides keeps nothing. All the rarities of his hunting life have gone to museums, mostly to the Coryndon at Nairobi, where he visits them from time to time, standing before the cases and dreamingly gloating. He likes to see them there and they give him no trouble. He would rather burn them with his own hands, I believe, than spend a moment of his life on the cares of maintenance, or waste a thought on the battle against moths and weevils.

One of the great virtues of the absence of possessions is

that attention is left free and perception sharpened. Ionides' attention, for the things that interest him, is perennially fresh; he can pass in a flash from an almost trance-like state of vacancy to a disciplined and active concentration. No living creature is too small for his curiosity, which is perhaps the reason, apart from idleness, why he does nothing to check the armies of cockroaches and ants which share the spare amenities of his house. The cockroaches hunt the kitchen and larder at night and rush down the well of the lavatory when disturbed, like demons returning to the pit, and by day the termites, tiny, white, transparent, whole disciplined armies, carry out excavations in the wooden window-frames, opening jagged crevices of daylight behind his head. The sugar ants, brown as cinnamon, confine themselves to the outside walls and the veranda, where they mine the cement, open trenches, and carry out systematic demolition. If there were bigger game to be watched he would of course prefer it; but the large romantic animals of Africa, apart from snakes, are scarce in this area, and he sees no reason to despise even the least prepossessing fauna.

There were things on the walls which startled me at first, especially in the evening in the uncertain lamplight, which cast strange shadows, but as soon as I found I had only to ask for information, or better still to capture a specimen, the nightly adventure of going from one room to another with a lantern became full of wary possibilities. There was a little dove-grey mottled lizard with dark eyes, a common house gecko, which appeared with fanatical punctuality every night on exactly the same patch of my bedroom wall. Once identified, and the serious business of his insect-hunting explained, he became a friendly feature of the night's routine; if he had ever absented himself I should have missed him. (His charming name in Swahili is *mjusi kafiri*, 'the unbeliever', as distinct from the two-striped skink, *mjusi islami*, which, as his holier name suggests, is a frequenter of mosques.) And there were other apparitions, more grotesque, which disconcerted me when I first saw them, but which, if I could bring them into the circle of lamplight for Ionides, proved to be known characters about the place, with their own idiosyncrasies and virtues. Most horrifying to my inexperience was a whip-scorpion which manifested each night on the wall of the unlit lavatory and was like nothing I had ever seen, a wickedly black and alert presence on the plaster, something between a spider and a bat. I retreated hurriedly at the first encounter, but on being mildly told to bring it in, went back with a tumbler and a piece of cardboard, using the cunning I had learned as a child, when wasps infested the kitchen during jam-making. Seen in the light this blackly sinister creature lost none of its menace; the body, a complex of carapace and legs, was only about the size of half-a-crown, but it deployed a pair of six-inch whip-like antennae which it cast about in an intelligent questing manner, like a dry-fly fisherman. These appendages were strong and stiff for the first inch, like the handle of a whip; then came a joint, and a long flexible lash which was rarely still. The front legs were not unlike a lobster's claws, folded tight at the elbow like a sprung trap and armed with polished cusps as sharp as pincers. The flat body, which on the shadowy wall had seemed as black as jet, now revealed a pattern of meticulous checker-board design in brown and black, evolved through what unimaginable processes of trial and error perhaps only an entomologist could guess. Even for a spider—for that I suppose is what the creature was—it seemed to have reached an absolute of strangeness, living in holes, making no web, detecting the footfall of a fly through its tremulous whip-lash, seizing its prey with unholy speed, living by all the strategies of the hunter. Not even the real scorpions, which from time to time crept out from the logs on the hearth, were as strange as this; nor the praying mantises which arrived inexplicably out of nowhere and turned their triangular heads and great green eyes in our direction, raising their arms in the famous 'spectral attitude' when menaced and sailing off into the shadows if one tried to touch them. The whip-scorpion I returned to his place when we had examined him, leaving him in the dark; but the implications of the experience were evidently not lost on him, for I never saw him again.

The place was full of life if one had eyes to see; none of it was big or dramatic, but one got a sense that though man has done his best to exterminate all the bigger mammals of Africa and keep a barren wilderness for himself, a teeming life continues there in spite of him, moving with cunning and stealth and out of sight. We rarely went out at night, but whenever we did a jackal would trot silently away from the rubbish-heap and green eyes would return the flash of our quavering headlights. One day while we were out snake-catching, a Temminck's pangolin, the scaly ant-eater, was surprised in the tangle of bushes behind the house, and tied with a piece of string until we got home. Ionides was not pleased with this interference and let it go, but I was glad of the chance of seeing it, for they are becoming rare, and would now be extinct if they were not protected. Its scales, strong and woody like the scales of a date-palm, are in great demand as charms, making it profitable to kill the creature, whose only defence is to roll up in a ball like a giant hedgehog and wait with stoic patience until the emergency is over. It is a slow walker, and was plodding about methodically at the end of its string when we came up to it, rising from time to time on its hind legs and moving horizontally, front paws tucked up as though in a muff, balancing itself by the weight of its heavy tail; but as soon as we tried to release the string it rolled into a scaly sphere like a wooden football and was impossible to unroll. The muscular strength controlling each scale is so powerful that it is easy to get one's fingers pinched as the scales clamp down like lids all over the body, and after rolling him gently over and failing to prise him apart we had to content ourselves with cutting off the string where we could see it, leaving him to uncoil himself at leisure. Ionides would not leave him without making a conspicuous mental note of the identity of the Africans present, and uttering threats as to what would happen if the pangolin were molested. Their smiles faded, and we left them shifting from foot to foot, visibly crestfallen.

There was no prohibition, however, about giant chameleons, save only that they must be left for Ionides to catch, an injunction willingly obeyed, since few Africans will touch these harmless creatures. We would often be sitting indoors in the afternoon, snake-catching over for the day, when word would come that someone had spotted a chameleon, and we would walk out with military speed to some nearby tree to find the reptile calm and contemplative above us. Their appearance alone is responsible for their evil reputation, for they move with a dreamlike slowness and have no defence but a hard and toothless bite. Once disturbed they will begin a stately climb to a safer position, opening their mouths in a roaring hiss and swivelling their strange eyes backward towards the pursuer. It was touching to see the confident lack of haste with which they went up hand over hand, coiling their tail at each step round the bending branch as Ionides carefully pulled it within reach. He taught me the way to take them, in a firm grip along the ridge of the back, using both hands and snatching the animal off the branch by surprise. They go flat at once, like an empty pouch, all the breath knocked out of them, and twist, slowly as ever, reaching for one's wrists with corkscrew tail and with leathery palms wide open. Their claws are sharp and long and their grip powerful; it is unwise to let them get a hold, for they can break the skin, and Rashidi's technique, which never fails to deceive, is to grasp the two hind feet and give them to each other, when they clasp together in a slow-motion handshake and give no further trouble. Their reactions are so slow that it is a miracle they have not been exterminated, especially among people like the Makua tribe, who will eat anything; only the spell of their appearance saves them, the magical stare, the fluted pie-crust frill along the back, the menacing lack of haste with which they place one careful hand before the other, opening their pointed mouths in a breathy roar. Their rage on finding themselves captured was slow to manifest, but very serious; they would gradually change their tint from bright to dark, turning an angry slate-colour as they twanged the wires of their cage, for days refusing our offerings of cockroaches.

The pleasantest sharer of our cramped quarters was a slender brown snake about five feet long, a hissing sand-snake (so called, Ionides explained, with the field-naturalist's irreverence for the systematist, because it was rarely found in sand and never hissed) which he picked up one morning as she lay sunning herself at the door of a native hut. She was not wanted for any collection, but she would be amusing to tame, being small and pretty and only mildly venomous. When we had tamed her we would let her go; in the meantime handling her, he thought, would give me confidence. This snake was a young female, with narrow head and full dark eyes and scales so smooth they felt like polished ivory. The Swahili name of this species is *kisanga*, which means simply 'sand snake', but which to English ears has a pretty sound and perfectly suited her. We kept her in a wire-fronted box beside my chair, and began the taming process in the early morning of the day following her capture. Diurnal snakes grow cold and torpid during the night and are comparatively indifferent to handling; when he took her out of her box and put her in my hands she remained in her flat coils like a polished ammonite, only raising her bird-like head after a pause and flickering her tongue over my hands in a drowsy effort to discover what was happening. The head with its round and jewel-like eye, dark pupil in a topaz ring, was delicate, from the fine scales like feathers clothing the neck to the pointed muzzle and tiny polished nostrils. She seemed to like the warmth of my hands, where she lay in apparent comfort across spread fingers and remained docile while I stroked her head and throat with a cautious forefinger. But as my warmth began to invade her she suddenly loosened, expanding concentric rings with an effortless movement and pouring outwards and away from the edge of my hand. She hung there swaying for a moment, flickering her tongue, the coils disengaging themselves on my palm and sliding apart with a smooth surge of muscle. I could feel her weight, and the rowing movement of ribs under the skin. In another moment, now fully alert, she would have dropped through my open fingers to the floor and I should have lost her; but Ionides' hand and wrist were under her head and she transferred herself to him in a leisurely progress. This was enough, he said; she must return to her box; much handling in the early stages would make her nervous.

After breakfast, when the air was warmer, we lifted her again, and this time she was aware of us, and active. Held in my lap, she would glide to my knee and project her body laterally through the air, then purposefully lower herself in a swinging curve, flickering her tongue and beginning to pour away. Ionides showed me how to place my hands alternately under the seeking head, deceiving her into feeling she made progress; but after a time she would grow tired of this, or would feel a timid suspicion that all was not well, when she would snatch herself backwards into a tense 'S', expressionless gaze upon us, tongue whipping in and out like a moist thread, body poised in the alert, the threatening position. 'She's nervous,' said Ionides, extending a slow hand and gathering her gently together into a skein. He put her back in the box a second time, gave her a tin of water and closed the lid, leaving her to sway about and explore the roof and at last to wrap herself over and round the water-tin, in what seemed a grotesquely comfortless position.

From then on, it became a habit to take her out of her

box as soon as we appeared, a flat, cold, coiled pancake of snake which we would cradle on our laps or hold in our arms until the warmth of our bodies stirred her into life. The first movement was always a faint pulsing or expanding, as the ribs began a gentle rise and fall, infinitely slow and tentative, like a magical quickening at the heart of something inanimate. Then the knot, threaded and looped through itself in a complex skein, would steadily draw apart, would loosen and expand till the bright head appeared, feeling its way with caution into the air, coil passing over coil in a smooth unfolding.

Since she was not to be sent away, and would stay with us as long as we chose to keep her, there was soon the problem of food to be considered. She did not look as though she had recently fed, and the tamer she got the more restless she became, especially when we ventured to take her out in the hot sun at the end of the veranda, when she would glide deliberately up to my neck and shoulders, rearing her elegant head to stare, as though she were expecting something. Ionides concluded that she was hungry. At first we proffered a succulent cockroach or two, which the cook was always able to produce, introducing them into her cage in the early morning; but these she treated with contempt; their scuttling presence seemed to irritate her. What she wanted, Ionides said, was a live lizard, and he went to some trouble to catch one of suitable size from a tree in the garden.

It was a pretty little thing, much darker than my bedroom gecko, with a rich brown stripe along either side of the body. It was in fact one of the lizards of the true faith, a mosque-lover, and I was afraid when I first saw it that it was one I had got to know rather well and which made a fat living out of one of the butterfly-traps in the garden. These traps were simple affairs, enamel plates suspended from a branch and covered with tents of cotton netting, like old-fashioned meat-covers. There was a gap between the plate and the bottom of the net, so that butterflies could comfortably walk in and gorge on the mess of banana with which the trap was baited. When full they would fly instinctively upwards, into the top of the net, where a careful hand could be introduced to take them. Ionides is not a butterfly expert, but was on the watch for a particular species to oblige an entomologist of his acquaintance. We rarely found what he was looking for, but would examine the traps each day and release the captive butterflies which were not wanted. It was a good place for sun-bathing; I would lie on a blanket in the afternoons and watch the traps, and discovered that I was not the only one to take an interest in them. There was a fat little two-striped skink who was usually sunning himself in a crevice of bark when I came from the veranda. He would disappear in a flash, with an audible rustle, but presently, when I had lain quite still for a time, first his hands and then his inquiring head would reappear, and when he had satisfied himself that I was asleep or unconscious he would proceed inch by inch down the tree and give his expert attention to the butterflies. He was impressive to watch, for the feat he performed was complicated, clearly the result of long and intelligent practice. The first step was to run smoothly along the twig from which the trap was suspended, and then, hand over hand like a sailor in reverse, to climb down the shrouds. Once arrived on the roof of the net, making it swing slightly, he would take a long look through the mesh at the delicious butterflies and run down the outside wall to the edge of the plate. The butterflies had little hope once he was inside, for he was very much quicker than they were, and also hungry. If he were feeling sufficiently confident he would dine where he was, choking down small specimens with hasty convulsive movements of head and neck, but more often, if he had caught a meal of a better size, would return the way he had come, legs and wings sticking out from both sides of his mouth, like a fox carrying a pheasant. He was so expert in his proceedings, so fat and glossy, so evidently on to a good thing and making the most of it, that I found myself watching him daily with increasing sympathy, and was dismayed when I thought he had been captured for the hungry sand-snake.

But it was not this merry burglar that had been brought in, only a small relation, and at first I watched its introduction into the snake-box without misgiving. But panic is a painful thing to observe, however small, and I never saw terror so eloquently expressed as in the desperate antics of this little creature. It flew round the walls of the cage like one possessed, hid behind the water tin, scrabbled to conceal itself beneath the snake, dashed out again in horror at the contact, wildly flitting from place to place in search of a cranny of safety from its devourer.

At first the snake regarded it with interest, and we hoped she would strike quickly and put an end to the spectacle; but she did nothing; only flinched occasionally when the lizard, keeping up its mad racket round the sides of the box, landed on some part of her body by mistake. At last she became bored and ignored the intruder, which by this time had decided that the safest thing was to hang by its toes from the underside of the lid, where it remained for the rest of the day, keeping a hypnotized watch on the enemy as she coiled herself for sleep. Each morning, for three successive days, we hoped to find that the lizard had disappeared, and that a bulge would tell us the snake had finally fed; but each day the life and death drama was still in progress, with the snake watchful or indifferent, and the lizard clinging inside the water-tin or crammed behind it, frantic as ever in its interminable hide-and-seek. After the third day Ionides, who had disliked the lizard's martyrdom as much as I had, and was resolute only in the interests of his snake, decided that she was not seriously hungry and that the skink had had enough. He pulled it out from behind the tin, the lizard all the time struggling and clasping his thumb with both hands, evidently believing its last hour had come, and tossed it down in the grass below the veranda. We both felt disproportionately relieved, and were glad when he discovered the reason for the snake's indifference. Her eyes, which had been always dark, one of her chief beauties, were seen to be covered with a milky film, opaque as two pearls, and this, he said, showed that she was about to slough and would not feed until the process was finished. Sure enough, after a few days of this milky blindness, accompanied by a dry and dull appearance over most of her body, we found her one morning as though born anew, shining and smooth, her dark gaze restored, while along the floor of the box lay a papery ghost, the old dress she had cast off unobserved, which I was sentimental enough to preserve in the pages of a book.

Not all the snakes were such pleasant house-companions, though they all contributed to our entertainment. The biggest gaboon viper, an immense female of great weight and stupendous lethargy, spent a fortnight instead of the usual week in our company, Ionides having decided that she was either gorged or pregnant, and being dubious about sending her off on her travels in either condition. She never appeared to move during those two weeks, but lay in majestic opulence against the wire, her sumptuous curves making a bulge in the netting. In the next box were three young males, whom her proximity seemed to make restless. They swelled and hissed, angrily wreathing about on one another, jabbing their blunt muzzles against the wire and flickering their supple tongues over the mesh. Their eyes had the steady brightness of yellow glass, and it was difficult to settle to conversation with this rhythmic ballet continually in progress. Finally, for the sake of peace, they had to be separated, and spent the rest of the week in different compartments, where their sexual rivalry, if such it was, subsided. The female maintained an immense indifference throughout and was finally packed up and sent to America with the rest, Ionides having decided that she was manifesting a false pregnancy, like Joanna Southcott, and had had time to get a grip on her digestion.

We kept only one green mamba in a cage, for not more than a few days, since I thought it a pity to contemplate nothing but the big vipers and puff-adders while the mambas lay out of sight, shrouded in calico. Ionides was at first unwilling for the experiment, not liking the idea of so active a snake in a lidded box which either I or the boys might absent-mindedly open. A mamba loose in the living-room, in spite of the stories invented about him, is something he says only a lunatic would risk, and for this reason he denies himself the pleasure of watching them. He agreed only on condition that the box were padlocked, and since I was able to produce a lock from my luggage, shook the snake cautiously out of its bag into the cage, locked it, and kept the key in his trousers pocket. The mamba came out of its trance in a moment, and for several days regaled us with its sinuous diversions. Its elegance and colour make it surely the most beautiful of its kind; as Ionides says, the aristocrat of snakes.

Some others were far from aristocratic in their behaviour, and one in particular, a singularly irritable puff-adder, seemed bent on causing the maximum embarrassment. It hissed atrociously whenever I passed, coiling convulsively backwards into the striking position and following me with a pale and baleful gaze. I never got used to the suddenness of this reaction, and would jump every time it happened, flinching absurdly out of my course between chair and table. Its eyes were steadily malevolent, as pale as moonstones, set in unwinking concentration; it swelled and deflated with a hiss whatever we did, even if we so much as laughed or struck a match. It was intolerable. It finally went too far in its demonstrations, and I was moved to complain. I emerged from my bedroom one morning to find Ionides peacefully smoking in his chair, surrounded by a stench which had already assailed me half-way up the passage. I had never encountered anything like it before; an evil sulphurous presence, the breath of the pit. I could not even return Ionides' greeting, but could only gasp and exclaim. He raised his eyebrows, apparently quite unconscious of any change, and turned his eyes benignly to the cages. 'I'm afraid,' he said, his tone measured and considerate as ever, 'that one of the big snakes must have defecated. Do you mind it, much? It'll pass off after a time. I'm afraid I no longer notice it.'

I did my best not to notice, but the room was hot, the nights being now so cold that we had a fire in the morning and ate our breakfast close to the blaze, in fierce comfort. I sat down to the table, but the air was as thick as fog, and when Makanga trailed in, stirring a cup of coffee, he was told that to oblige the *mama* one of the snakes must be changed to a clean box. It was, needless to say, the puff-adder, which was now noticeably thinner. Doors were opened for the sake of air, a box was brought and the culprit transferred to the clean one without mishap. Ionides returned to the table and his cooling sausage. But the miasmal box was left on the floor beside me, exhaling a breath incompatible with breakfast, and Makanga had to be recalled and told to remove it—could I believe my ears?—'into the larder'. There it remained for the next day or two, and either the offensiveness passed off, as I was told it would, or I grew accustomed to it, for it troubled me no more. But I did, at my next Swahili lesson with Ionides, learn an expression which I addressed with malice to the unspeakable puff-adder, '*Unanuka, mama*', which means, with all directness, 'Mother, you stink' (for the snake, I am sorry to say, was undoubtedly a female); a rebuke which convulsed Makanga with simple merriment.

V

DOMESTIC COMPLICATIONS

SETTLED as his life had seemed when I arrived to disturb it, I soon found that Ionides was uneasy about the future. Living in Tanganyika, as in many African countries at this moment of history, is like living in the territory of an apparently benign but incalculable magician. Anything, one feels, may happen; the laws of cause and effect may no longer apply; at any moment an unlucky word may be spoken or a spell break; a change come over the air and invisible necromancies be set in motion. Ionides loathes politics and in the past has kept them out of his life with singular success, reading no newspapers, owning no radio, being quite content with the hearsay of occasional cronies. But nowadays politics break in even on the most enclosed lives, and nobody knows which way the country will go. European pessimists, disgruntled civil servants whose careers have been brought to an end by *Uhuru* (independence), are apt to believe that after a feverish few years, with or without bloodshed, the economy of the country will collapse and some of it, or most, revert to bush. Educated Tanganyikans, who are not as numerous as the new republic could wish, take naturally a different view; as they see it, the disappearance of the white man (and later, one suspects, of the industrious Indian), will initiate a golden age of development and prosperity in which Africans will enjoy the rewards of which they have long been defrauded. What the uneducated think, the vast majority, none can tell, nor does it appear that anyone greatly cares. They accept what they are told and go on with the business of living, which for the most part is precarious enough to occupy their whole attention. All that reaches them is a tenuous and variable thread of communication which sometimes produces results, one must suppose, very different from what the government intended.

Ionides loves Tanganyika, in which he has spent nearly forty years of his life, and though his reactionary spirit ('that perfectly honourable and legitimate instinct, the love of the *status quo*', as Henry James once put it), prevents him from regarding the British exodus with enthusiasm, he had until recently no other thought but to stay there to the end. He had even taken out papers for Tanganyikan citizenship (disobligingly explained in private—'Now the British Empire's come to an end I'd just as soon be a Hottentot') and showed a friendly interest in the new African administrators (John Ambrose, the newly appointed District Commissioner at Newala for example), with whom he came in contact. But an incident had occurred which had undermined his confidence and upset him, causing him to retaliate in wrath by cancelling his application for citizenship.

The disturbance had happened only a few days before I arrived in Newala, and concerned his servants. Ionides, as I have said, employs eight, four for the snake-catching, four for the running of his household, and had always, by current standards, paid them generously. For the past three years Abdullah Makabui, his major-domo, had had two hundred shillings a month; the cook, Majingililo, a hundred and eighty. Makanga the house-man got a hundred and forty a month; Yassini, the caretaker, whose duties were light and consisted of squatting on the veranda if we were out at night and keeping watch on the house when Ionides was on safari, a hundred and twenty. (I give these details for the sake of local comparison; it would be quite unrealistic to compare them with European standards.) On the same scale Mustapha, the driver of the Land Rover, to whom the engine was a mystery and who had no mechanical knowledge, was paid two hundred and thirty shillings a month, the same as Ahmadi, the lorry driver, who could change a plug if he must; while the two snake-hands, Rashidi and Pétu, got a hundred and sixty and a hundred and thirty shillings respectively. If these wages sound meagre it must be remembered that each of them got a free house, free firewood from the property and free water—this last a considerable item, since every drop is drawn from Ionides' tap and paid for on his meter. As well as this they plant their crops on his land and sell the harvest from his cashew trees, which is not a universal custom. Detailed comparisons of wages would be wearisome, and it is enough to say that the cook employed by his nearest European neighbour (a much better cook than Majingililo, who by any but Ionides' standards would be unemployable) gets exactly half the money, while the drivers employed by the Makonde Water Corporation and the Government Game Department get a flat rate of a hundred and fifty shillings.

By all accounts they considered themselves well off, almost a little local aristocracy. They do not belong to any of the local tribes but to the Wangindo, who are settled round Liwale, Ionides having brought them from his first home when he moved to Newala. They keep themselves pretty much to themselves, all of them, with the exception of Pétu, who married a local girl, having brought their wives with them from further north. They live in a little community of cottages a hundred yards or so from Ionides' house, far enough for him not to hear their radios or their children, near enough for them to answer a summons when he gives one of his formidable yells. He had always maintained a fatherly relation to all of them, and had made provision for them in his will. Now, for the first time, there was trouble. A spectacled African arrived, tidily dressed in jacket and trousers with a pocketful of fountain-pens (the uniform, it seems, of the trouble-maker) and had privately interviewed Ionides' employees, eliciting the details of their wages and instructing them that they must strike for more. This was the local representative of the Transport and General Workers' Union, and his word carried weight. He had not, apparently, consulted the District Commissioner or made any local comparison of wages before taking action, and the first Ionides knew of his activities was when his team presented him with an ultimatum. Anger succeeded astonishment, but he was in a cleft stick and knew it. Without his trained helpers, whom he had taught himself, the snake-catching could not be carried on, and habit had long attached him to his personal servants. He savagely revised the wage-scale from top to bottom, Makabui's money being raised by fifty per cent and the others receiving an increase in proportion. He was now paying at a vastly higher rate than anyone else in the neighbourhood, and could afford no more; but he now believed that he had been singled out for experiment, and that this was only the beginning of a concerted plan of 'blackmail and extortion'. Sure enough, in the course of a week or two 'our spectacled friend', as we cautiously described him in conversation, made a second appearance in the compound and was seen in earnest conference with the drivers, making notes. He did on this occasion send a message that he wished to speak to Ionides, who refused to receive him, maintaining that he had done all he could and that further discussion would be a waste of time and temper. After this second visit he gave himself up to foreboding, and for many sleepless nights, while his cough grew alarmingly worse, distastefully turned over plans for leaving Tanganyika.

It was the implications of the business that distressed him, threatening, as they seemed to do, the prospects of life for Europeans in the future. Tanganyika has had, on the whole, as good an administrative history under British rule as anywhere in Africa; perhaps better than most; relations between black and white had seemed always friendly. On all sides one heard it said that Tanganyika was fortunate in having so remarkable a leader as Julius Nyerere, adored by Africans, warmly liked and admired by the outgoing administration, a man who would bring his country into the modern world with the maximum of tolerance and intelligence. His renunciation of the premiership had been a shock, and nobody knew what to make of it; but the new Prime Minister, Rashidi Kawawa, was an able man of attractive personality, and the prevailing feeling was one of optimism. If any African country could negotiate a smooth passage into freedom, preserving good relations between black and white, that country was Tanganyika. (For Rashidi Kawawa Ionides had a distinctly partial feeling, for his father had been one of his game scouts in the old days, and he remembered the boy as outstandingly promising, small and cheerful, with a comic gift for mimicry. On my first night in Dar-es-Salaam, newly arrived from England, I had dined with Mr. Kawawa at his house, and he had recalled those carefree days with pleasure, laughing a great deal over stories of Ionides and his father.)

Since then, however, disturbing rumours had filtered through to Newala. Africanisation was of course proceeding everywhere apace, as was to be expected, and British Civil Servants were preparing to leave, with as good a grace as they could muster; but those other Europeans who had long felt wedded to the country and had had no thought of uprooting themselves were said to be drifting away reluctantly, in great numbers. Most of the European doctors had already left Dar-es-Salaam, leaving their practices to Africans and Indians. Farms were being sold, legal and commercial practices given up, all contributing to a growing atmosphere of belief that a European community was no longer wanted.

Ionides now felt, rightly or wrongly, that as Newala's

only European celebrity he had been deliberately singled out for special treatment. His snake-catching, with its daily payments of money all over the area, had the status of a little local industry, and since the district is poor and life precarious it would clearly be advantageous to keep him there. But the legend that he is a rich man who is making a handsome fortune out of African snakes is generally believed, and the assumption seemed to be that while no one would wish him to leave, it would be only common sense to put the screws on. Pressure had already been twice applied, and there was no guarantee that this would be the last of it. One of the snake-hands and one of the drivers had responded to the situation with some eagerness, and there was a mutter of gossip to the effect that, if he did decide to go, they would of course supply the zoos of the world without him. Such ignorant talk did nothing to improve his temper, and in the early days of my visit we spent much time in discussing the possibility of his moving to another part of Africa. From his point of view there was only one meagre argument in favour: he had sometimes felt that, so far as snakes were concerned, he had 'caught out' the area, and would find it more interesting to be dealing with a greater variety of species. The question was, where? With almost the whole of Africa in a state of political turmoil it was difficult to think of a country where one could settle down to snake-catching undisturbed. Besides, from his base in Newala he had always been free to move into Kenya or Uganda when the lust for carpet-vipers overtook him, and these lengthy safaris of several months at a time had long been part of the pattern of his life. To retire, to return to England, was out of the question. He said quite frankly that he would rather be dead. On the other hand, if this were the beginning of the usual political syndrome, if there were to be eavesdropping and reporting, with penalties imposed for sentiments privately expressed (we had already heard of some examples) which official zeal could interpret as 'insulting the Tanganyika flag', then there was little comfort in deciding to stay. 'If I've got to look round furtively before I express an opinion, I'd rather leave the country.'

We found ourselves looking round furtively already, and with good reason, for the reporting of conversations is a popular sport and never more so than in a politically backward country. There had been the usual stories in the newspapers of Europeans deported at a few days' notice for remarks overheard in bars in Dar-es-Salaam, and now, from John Knight, the Agricultural Officer at Newala, we were getting details of the trouble which had overtaken Martin Symonds, the Agricultural Officer in charge of the experimental farm at Nachingwea. This man was described as a mild, pacific type, wrapped up in his job and with no interest in politics. He had been away on long leave and had returned to the farm in January, to find everything very slack under the African field officer, with certain abuses going merrily unchecked. In this country, where anthrax is rampant, it is a rule of all government farms that when an animal dies of disease it must be buried. During his absence a number of cattle had mysteriously died and had been handed over to the labour force for food. He had arrived in time to find the latest carcase being skinned and jointed, and had confiscated it, blowing up the clerk in charge for this breach of regulations. This was the beginning of some very uneasy proceedings. Police askaris carried out investigations during three days, interviewing the labour force and accusing Martin Symonds of using abusive language to the clerk, and, of course, insulting the flag on unspecified occasions. The police had eventually withdrawn their charges, but three months later orders had come from the Attorney General's office, instructing them to prosecute. This prosecution, now pending, was an extremely serious matter for Symonds, since conviction would mean the end of his career and probably deportation. We were waiting with some misgiving for the result; the evidence was not expected to be of high ethical quality, the labour force having been formed, we were told, largely from the unemployed of Dar-es-Salaam, sent out to Nachingwea under a resettlement scheme and consequently displeased and discontented. Anti-European feeling rather than any legitimate grievance against the Agricultural Officer seemed to be at the bottom of the disturbance, which did not help us to feel sanguine about the future. Since then, of course, a Preventive Detention Bill has been passed, allowing for imprisonment without the formality of charges, the Bill being explained as desirable 'to protect freedom'—a nice example of the way in which political usage reconditions meaning. But the charge against Symonds, I am glad to say, eventually got short shrift in the magistrate's court, being dismissed on account of the ludicrous contradictions in the evidence.

We had become rather wary in our talk when we were not alone, for there was something about the monotonous morning trips in the Land Rover which stimulated conversation, and as I was always wedged in between Ionides and the driver, with the snake-hands and other occupants piled up against our shoulders, our shouted exchanges were naturally common property. It was fairly safe to assume that nobody spoke English, but not entirely so, for Ionides' men could recognize a word here and there when they heard it and could fill in the rest by guesswork. It was unwise to mention names; the pricking of ears when we did so was almost audible, and we soon devised a system of code names and expressions which we hoped would effectively scramble the conversation. Thus the union official became 'our spectacled friend', and *Uhuru*, the comprehensive term for the new *régime*, was by a happy inspiration changed to '*upupu*'. *Upupu* is the Swahili name of the buffalo bean, a devilish climbing plant which, when touched, shakes off a shower of poisonous hairs which cause a severe though fortunately temporary irritation. It was natural, since we all encountered it from time to time, that this disagreeable plant should be occasionally mentioned, but its frequency in our conversation must, to an eavesdropping ear, have seemed extraordinary. 'Now that we have *upupu* . . . since *upupu* was declared I must confess I have noticed . . . goodness knows what the *upupu* decision will be on such and such a point . . .' and so on. We discussed it for hours, sometimes catching a bewildered expression on the faces of our companions, as though confronted with the idea that as well as taking an interest in snakes I must also be passionately curious about botany.

The ruse served well enough, and we were able to say, within limits, what we wished, gravely exchanging ribaldries which it would have been agony to suppress, and more than unwise to have uttered in Swahili. Though he was full of sympathy for the civil servants who were losing their jobs, many of them after half a lifetime of service, and sorry for the other Europeans who, mostly for the sake of their children's future, thought it expedient to leave, Ionides was scornful of the sentimental complaints that one occasionally heard. Protests about the best years of one's life and the ingratitude of Africans left him contemptuously cold. What had they come to Tanganyika for, he would argue, if not 'in the lively expectation of favours to come'? Those who claimed to have dedicated themselves to an alien people, and expected gratitude, had failed to observe nature. In the human as in the animal world, ingratitude was the rule; it was hypocrisy to pretend otherwise. 'I've asked many of them why they first came out here, and there hasn't been one that didn't come out for a career. It's called, I know, "dedicating oneself to the African", but that wasn't the original motive. They came as I did, because it suited them, and now that it doesn't suit the African any more it's ridiculous to moan about ingratitude. I haven't much time for hypocrisy have you? Wouldn't politics be more respectable without it?' Certainly ingratitude is never one of his own complaints, however violent his annoyance over the possibility of having to uproot himself. He and his Africans, he would say, have been mutually useful to one another, and it is a pity—he would use no stronger word—if for no good reason the relationship has to end. Even the grasping attitude towards Europeans, which has become so popular under *upupu* and of which he now feels himself to be the victim, is, he claims, wholly the fault of the Europeans themselves. When he had first come to Africa to pursue his life in the bush, chiefs and villagers alike had been courteous and helpful, following the unsophisticated rule that the stranger befriended today may befriend one tomorrow. Now nobody did anything, even telling a stranger the way, without expecting payment; it was 'nowt for nowt for nobody', and this was an entirely European conception. The noble savage was laughed at as a sentimental figment, but there had been some truth in it. If nowadays the African seemed to expect everything for nothing, and to be chary of goodwill, we had only ourselves to blame for the corruption.

Towards Africans themselves, as people to live among, his attitude is uncomplicated and friendly. He is always surprised when people ask him, as they sometimes do, how he manages to live so happily in solitude. 'Solitude? I suppose it's a word one uses for want of a better. I'm never lonely. I'm surrounded by Africans. I've never experienced solitude; I wouldn't face a dark cell any better than anyone else.' He will even admit, if pressed, that the strongest attachment of his life has been to an African, Issa Mtandu, his old cook, who served him in confidence and friendship for nineteen years and whom he loved as a brother. Mtandu had been a much married man, with no fewer than sixteen wives at one time and another, but to his grief had remained childless. He had gone with Ionides to the war, and after twenty months' absence from Tanganyika had been touchingly pleased to hear that one of his younger wives had borne him a child. Simple arithmetic, obligingly worked out for him by his companions, did nothing to spoil his pleasure in the news. 'What is the difference?' he had said, 'a child is a child'; and Ionides had loved him for his tolerance. After the war, on a long gorilla-hunting trip in the Congo, Mtandu had fallen mysteriously ill. He was a heavy drinker, which perhaps was the cause of his obscure disease; nobody ever knew. He had been carried into hospital and died there, leaving Ionides bereft in a way that shocked him. For more than a year he had failed to shake off his grief, and this experience, so painful and unexpected, had determined him never to feel so deeply again. He accordingly maintains, or does his best to maintain, a philosophic detachment in all relationships, enjoying companionship wherever he finds it, without expecting it to last. This detachment is something that he achieves with difficulty, for he is an emotional Greek at heart, and in spite of his lonely life and his pretence of being indifferent to human beings, temperamentally and incurably gregarious.

He refers to himself often, mockingly, as 'Father', and one of his grievances against *upupu* is that it is bringing the paternal relationship to an end. His instincts are benevolently authoritarian; he is a patriarch without family, and resents the necessity to deal through official channels with problems which seem to demand only common sense. Some time before my arrival in Newala Pétu, the junior snake-hand, had provided one, and the early weeks were disturbed by its repercussions. This handsome young man, so apparently docile and quiet that I believe I never heard him utter a word, had a passionate streak in his nature which made him unpredictable. He was a jealous husband. Unlike the other seven he had married outside his tribe, and had a young wife who came from a Makonde village somewhere on the plateau. So far as anyone knew she had never given him the smallest cause for jealousy, but to minds infected by this mania in its pure form, as Pétu's apparently was, no pretext is necessary; the explosion takes place at rhythmic intervals and runs its dangerous course to the point of exhaustion. In the months before my arrival Ionides had been on safari in Kenya, accompanied by his servants with their wives and families. (This is a usual precaution and makes for harmony, for the Makonde women have an easy-going reputation and are not willingly left alone by careful husbands. John Knight's curious assertion that the local women were notoriously immoral while the men were the reverse had puzzled me at first, until I discovered that the puritanical strictness of the husbands, so seriously praised, consisted in frequenting only unmarried girls and prostitutes and leaving each other's wives alone, as being too dangerous.) On this particular safari, camping in an area where lions and leopards abounded, Pétu, overtaken by one of his emotional cataclysms, had accused the cook, poor old Majingililo, that timid scarecrow, of casting lascivious glances at his wife. He had done nothing to Majingililo, but had beaten his wife so viciously that the other servants, hearing the uproar and the screams and spying on the wretched girl's extremity, had run to Ionides in alarm, begging him to intervene before she was murdered. Pétu was summoned and brought before him, trembling like one possessed, and out of breath. In the old days Ionides' discipline would have been sharp and swift, and Pétu would have had a dose of his own medicine; but nowadays summary justice is too risky; domestic violence is a matter for the police. 'I told him that it was not my practice to interfere between husband and wife, and that I took no interest in what they did to one another, but that causing her bodily harm was against the law, and I forbade him to touch her.' Pétu had listened with downcast eyes and replied, breathless but still respectful, that he would obey his master in everything that concerned him, but that this was no concern of his and he would do as he pleased. With that he wrenched himself free and ran back to his hut, where he resumed the frantic beating. The other servants, ordered to pursue and stop him, had stood sheepishly still, far too terrified to risk further interference, and before Ionides could get to the spot she had broken away from her husband and run off into the bush, where she remained, hiding and wandering in a deplorable condition, most of the night. At the end of this time she had been found, or had crept back to the camp, I do not remember which; and Pétu's rage had cooled; the fit was over. But the incident had alarmed and unsettled everybody, for not only had murder been narrowly avoided, but the poor woman, by escaping into the bush and hiding there, had run the risk of an equally horrible death. The situation was dangerous and would continue so, since Pétu's violence seemed a kind of madness, beyond the reach of reason. Now that the spell was over he listened with his usual good manners to Ionides' warnings, making no answer and returning each night to his hut in ominous silence, while the camp listened. The sensible course was obvious; the girl should return to her parents, which she was anxious to do; but here another difficulty arose, for the return of a wife implies the repayment of the bride-price to the husband, and for this the financially sensitive Makonde parents were unwilling. The average bride-price in these parts is two hundred shillings, normally paid in cash, and for want of this money, which would have meant parting with several goats, Pétu's wife must continue as she had begun.

The misery of her situation haunted my early days and nights in Newala, and I found it difficult to look at Pétu without anger, or to return his greeting. I could not believe that nothing could be done, but native custom and the girl's own helpless acceptance of her situation put an end to every rational suggestion. Makabui, the head servant, a man of great intelligence and charm, was all for submitting the case to the native court, which would have laid the evidence before the village elders and had authority to insist on separation. But Pétu's wife would not go before the court, being afraid that the mere proceeding would blast her reputation, and that to be turned away from her home and refused by her parents would be infinitely worse than staying where she was. This made it impossible for anyone to make a move on her behalf, committed as she was to the obstinate fatalism of African women. And their self-immolating patience is not as foolish as it sounds, for a divorced woman has usually no resource but prostitution. It is easy to make mistakes when dealing with a custom-bound society, as many Christian missionaries have discovered. Conversion to Christianity implies monogamy, all male converts being required to return the surplus wives and stick to one, with the result that in villages where Christianity has made progress there is also the greatest number of prostitutes. This is a problem for the missionaries, and I do not know how they justify it. Prostitution as a trade is not, generally speaking, despised in Africa; there is no stigma worth speaking of; but I doubt if the Church is much cheered by this redeeming feature.

Perhaps by this time Pétu's wife has come to terms with the hazards of marriage; I have not heard that the police have been called in, or any bones broken. While I was still at Newala she gave birth to a baby, which she must have been carrying at the time of the safari incident, and Pétu appeared for the first time in shoes, a particularly repulsive pair of plastic sandals. He had always gone barefoot before, and this, I learned, was a magical precaution observed for the sake of the child, one of the innumerable taboos surrounding the phenomena of birth, making them either dangerous or unclean. A man whose wife is pregnant is considered unclean until after the delivery; he is debarred from many activities and may not take part in a lion-hunt, not even in the rounding-up of a man-eater, since his presence among the hunters would invite disaster. If he presumes to wear shoes during this period his child may be born web-footed, or without toes; so that for all his disadvantages as a husband Pétu was presumably taking paternity seriously. After childbirth a woman is unclean for a much longer period; she is confined to her hut, allowed only certain foods, may not touch the belongings of others, and so on. This unattractive conception of the uncleanness of birth and sexual intercourse is almost universal among African peoples, and deeply mysterious; it seems to spring from a kind of horror, a buried fear which in civilized communities would be described as neurotic. Among the Makonde the period of taboo after childbirth, during which sexual intercourse is forbidden, lasts for two years, which one might explain as a primitive attempt at birth-control, wise in intention but in practice merrily defeated by polygyny. Certainly I never saw Pétu's wife again after the birth of her baby, which I often heard wailing, and could only hope that her new celibacy would sweeten her husband's temper and improve her lot; which is, I fear, doubtful.

VI

CONVERSATION ON THE RAVINE

EVENING comes early in Tanganyika and the dusk is brief; sunset is swiftly followed by the dark. Nearly every afternoon a wind awoke, rustling the leaves and driving over a procession of speeding clouds, so that the fierce sun which stung one's skin appeared and disappeared in a chequer-board sky, hot and cool by turns, with the whole sky in motion. Later this wind would die as abruptly as it came, the clouds would be carried away by their own momentum and the magic stillness of late afternoon begin. This was the time of birds and transformations, when we would walk slowly for half a mile from the house and sit on the edge of a ravine as at a spectacle. This dramatic gorge, a fissure in the very lip of the high plateau, was brilliant with crimson earth and rock in which a tangle of trees and scrub held precarious footing. It seemed to fascinate the birds, which sailed about at this hour above the abyss, rising and falling on waves of invisible currents. Ravens frequented this air in great numbers, swooping and turning in light-hearted acrobatics surely performed for pleasure, an audible rushing of wings going on below us and much raucous conversation as they answered one another across the gorge. They are handsome birds, with a startling band of white at the back of the neck and an elegant ivory tip at the point of the bill.

There is at least a pair nesting in every village and near any group of huts, arguing over scraps, inspecting the rubbish heaps in committee, patrolling the place with magisterial gait. In the afternoon the ravine was their aerial playground, and there was hardly a moment when there was not a black figure, rising, falling, twisting and turning in the gulf below or alighting heavily on a branch with ostentatious croaking. The doves would be all around us but invisible, hooting softly in those crescendos of eerie laughter which have earned the laughing-dove its name, and the two little sorts of black widow-bird, the paradise and the pin-tailed, would climb into the air from time to time and trace an erratic course like sooty comets. These have small bodies and long extravagant double-streamer tails, and I never tired of watching their curious flight, which for all their tininess appears to require great effort. The smaller widow-bird goes up in a light-hearted leaping ascent not unlike the lark's, its tail streaming out behind and seeming with its weight to check each mounting parabola. The paradise whydah has an even longer tail and its flight is clumsy; its progress is full of anxiety, a series of leaps through the air, dragging its comet feathers. Their performance was rudely mocked by the clowning ravens.

But the birds were not our only entertainment; the light itself at this hour was an exquisite drama. From where we sat, crouched on our heels on a patch of eroded earth from which bushes and roots had been swept by the April rains, we looked out across the further edge of the crevasse to a vast stretch of plain and distant hills, already filling their hollows with mauve shadow. Mist rose from the Ruvuma River like a tide and flowed out to the bases of those strange citadels of rock which millions of years of weathering have not scoured from the plain; pencils of smoke rose up from invisible cooking-fires, their topmost plumes in sunlight, while the crags to the west turned crimson and gold in the rays of an almost unbearable effulgence.

It would have been more than enough to sit in silence,

but this we rarely did; it was even better to talk on the brink of such splendours; they were a stimulus. Sometimes Ionides would regale me with stories from ancient history, of the commendable ingenuity of Hannibal, who 'about 202 B.C., if my memory serves me', surprised and seized the Roman fleet by rowing out to the ships at night with earthen pots full of vipers and tossing them on to the decks, where the pots broke and the vipers routed the crew. ('How did he happen to have the vipers about him?' 'He collected them, naturally.' 'And his own men weren't afraid of them, which seems strange?' 'History doesn't relate; one supposes that Hannibal, being an intelligent man, knew more about them than Scipio Africanus or his crews. It's a slow snake, as you've observed. But disconcerting, I dare say, to have let loose around one in great numbers in the middle of the night. Anyway, it worked.') Or he might speak, since we had touched on sailors, of their valuable knowledge of the stars (a pale star, the first and to me unknown, would by this time be faintly perceptible above us) and of how an unknown mariner had guided the British forces by the stars across the desert in 1882, to the battle of Tel-el-Kebir against Arabi Pasha, 'the Nasser of the period', and how the 17,000 British under Lord Wolseley had defeated the Egyptians, 22,000 strong, a victory which could never have been won if it had not been for that sailor and his constellations.

By this time, though I was happy to listen to the stories of any of his heroes (except Genghis Khan, whose very name was like a knell and who now was mentioned only by permission) I liked best to hear of Ionides' own adventures, which have all been of hunting and harsh and solitary experiments with life, each one contributing something to the man he has become. The mind of the obsessed hunter is so strange to me, so different in its processes from anything I could independently imagine, that I followed each clue as though it were a fragment of a puzzle which the next question and answer would push into place, bringing me nearer to a view of the whole pattern. How has he come to be the rarity that he is? What bizarre mutation has separated him from his kind, made him indifferent to their life, robbed their values of meaning, set him so purposefully apart in this pocket of Africa? In a sense his beginnings were English and conventional enough, though not his origins. He was born in a large Victorian house in Hove, second child and only son of a successful surgeon. He had learned misery the common way at a hated prep-school, and had gone through Rugby and Sandhurst and finally the army. How could this tame and conformist history have produced the man squatting on his heels on the red cliff beside me, grizzled and emaciated, brown as a walnut, his eyes lit up over reminiscences of poaching and tracking, of hardships and dubious escapades, the violent odyssey of a hunter? The foreign and incalculable thing about him is that he is a Greek, as his name implies. Though his is the fifth generation of the family to be born in England they have kept their Levantine blood remarkably pure; under the prosperous and established surface the essential difference, the foreignness, has not assimilated. He has always felt, or been made to feel himself, a foreigner, and conformity for him has no attraction. He is nonconformist by nature, and from that it is an easy step to being a rebel. Beyond that I find it impossible to account for any of his qualities; neither his family nor his upbringing seems to illuminate anything. The original family name, he says, was Ixplixsis, and he is not even certain whether it was Phanariot Greek or derived from the Turkish. He knows only that Ixplixsis being unmanageable in English it was at some point changed to Ionides, meaning 'the Greek', a nickname which pursued him all through his schooldays and youth and was shaken off only when he left the army and disappeared into Africa.

If one had invented Ionides, presenting him as a character in a novel, one would go wildly astray in one's efforts to make him credible. One would imagine an exotic childhood in some wild and tropical place, repressive parents, the shock of being uprooted and sent to England, the bitterness of school which turned him sour, the final experience (some deep emotional betrayal, surely, introducing a symbolic element) which left such a scar that he retired into defensive solitude, drinking hard, a haunted and embittered Conrad character. All of this, with the exception of the hated preparatory school, would be untrue; but to the reader accustomed to psychological equations the real facts of the case would be unconvincing. The scenes of childhood were no wilder and stranger than the sea-front at Brighton; his parents, though his father was a selfish man indifferent to children, were conventionally kind, and with his mother his relations were always memorably good. The sadistic beatings endured at school were certainly a shock, but curiously enough they quite failed to embitter him. They taught him fear, but he sets a value on fear, and if one can accept the paradox, is not afraid of it. And in spite of the occasional fierceness of his aspect and some of his behaviour, in innumerable ways he is the gentlest of men, manifesting a rare tenderness to children and animals. He rarely probes into his own nature (he calls this 'unhealthy') and though he admits the lessons he has learned from experience and profits by them, he is chary of peering too closely into motives. His gaze is always outward, away from himself, observing and recording. 'I believe in evading issues that are not likely to prove profitable.'

Where then did this single-minded passion for hunting come from, with its taste for hardship, freedom from distraction, the intensity of a manic concentration? His father enjoyed shooting and stalking in a gentlemanly way, even big-game hunting with all its costly and customary appurtenances; but that hobby was on a different scale, belonged to a different world, to the comfortable pastimes of an Edwardian gentleman. 'He always wanted jam on it,' is Ionides' comment. ('Jam', according to him, is something one must never demand from life. It stands for comfort, luxury, easy wish-fulfilment, for all the sugary trimmings of life that he prefers to forgo. If it comes his way by accident, well and good; the stoic rule is that one must never look for it.) His father's sporting tastes can hardly have been a determining influence, for he can never remember a time when the desire to pursue and capture some living treasure was not already so strong as to be irresistible. The earliest recollection of his life (he cannot have been more than five) is of being forbidden to climb a wall in pursuit of a Red Admiral butterfly, and of being punished by his nurse for persisting in doing so. The desire was already there, the persistence developed; the only difference now is that the hunter has evolved into the naturalist, the killer turned preserver; but it has taken half a lifetime.

If I were to make a guess at the driving force behind his single-mindedness I would say it is that same urge which moves poets, artists and many men of action—a lifelong thirst for intensity of experience. Ionides' thirst is a primitive one, concentrated and disciplined by intelligence. It is a passion for getting down to the bed-rock of existence, for meeting a challenge unaided, with every faculty at full stretch and life consciously felt through every sense because of the proximity of death. The satisfactions he has achieved are not, I believe, so very different from the release and exhilaration which many people find in danger and war, in the creation of works of art, in all solitary and difficult forms of self-expression. Like all artists he is egocentric. He could never have achieved the life he has led if he had felt (as we are all expected to feel nowadays) participation in communal life as a moral obligation. He belongs by temperament to an earlier age, when it was respectable, even praiseworthy, for a man to be primarily concerned with his own soul.

Intensity of experience is more difficult to achieve, and when achieved more heavily charged and precariously balanced, than sheer excitement. It is a sort of ecstasy, though this is a word Ionides would never use. In his experience the supreme moments have always been sharpened by fear, which seems necessary to bring his nerves to the last pitch of awareness. He does not attempt to explain this, beyond proposing a theory that it is a physical reaction common to all animals, and for which the adrenal gland is probably responsible; but he will candidly own it. He is a connoisseur of fear, which he has studied in himself and remembers from many occasions with painful vividness. It is not a sensation that he enjoys, but he is familiar with its features, has marked its curious ebb and flow in the presence of danger, and in the aftermath of languor and satisfaction which followed the most intense of his hunting experiences accepts it as having been a prime ingredient. Curiously enough—or perhaps it only seems curious in so extrovert a man—the most fearful experiences of his life have all been dreams. He does not expatiate on these; they seem chiefly to have been a backwash of imagination after an event which his consciousness was at the time too narrowly focused to perceive. Thus, on a famous occasion in the Lushoto district of Tanganyika, when he was mauled by a wounded elephant and narrowly escaped death, the dreams of the succeeding weeks were far more terrifying than even the worst moments of the actual encounter.

After dreams, he ranks the fears of his earliest years at school, before a beating, as the most insufferable. 'Nothing,' he says, 'nothing in adult life has been as bad as that. I can remember being so frightened that I was cold and sick, my knees knocking together, not being able to believe I should survive until the thing was over.' He had been eight and a half years old when he was sent to his preparatory school and subjected (he was a difficult boy) to this sadistic discipline; yet the only reproach he will make against either parents or school is that he was exposed to this ugly experience too young. It taught him, he says, two valuable lessons: that human beings are at heart more savage than animals, and that it is folly to expect justice in this world. (Justice, he maintains, is an artificial concept anyway, unheard of in nature—an attitude which successfully arms him against disappointment.) So that all in all, looking back, he concludes that his stormy years at school did him nothing but good, even taking into account the fact that, both at his preparatory school and at Rugby, he endured more beatings than one would expect to hear of outside the pages of a Victorian religious tract or a particularly nasty novel. But if one asks him, remembering his sympathy for children, whether he would expose a son of his own to the same rigours, he hesitates. He believes in sending boys to public school, and would be vastly impatient of the tender-minded ideas of educational progressives. But eight and a half is too young to turn any child adrift in that particular jungle; at that age a child should be still in the nest, its base should be home. 'I was too young,' he says, 'too vulnerable. My parents made an error of judgment, that was all. Later on it wouldn't have mattered.' Though the experience left its mark he feels only a mild detached regret; there is no trace of bitterness.

In his hunter's life he has experienced boredom, disappointment, privation, and of course fear, and has consistently taken 'nature notes' on all of them. This is not to say that he has recorded his reactions; 'nature notes' is simply his name for an independent and lifelong habit of observation, both of animals and men, whom he normally differentiates as 'human animals'. His own response to fear has interested him as a natural phenomenon, and he has had abundant opportunity of noting its different stages and variations. The most frightening experience for a hunter, he says, is being alone on the track of a dangerous wounded animal. 'I used to think that the elephant was the most frightening of all, but this was a subjective impression, not supported by reason. I think I believed it originally because the man who first introduced me to elephant-hunting told me some hair-raising stories; I suppose he thought that being ignorant I would probably be reckless. Then of course there's the huge size and apparent irresistibility of the beast, and the ominous noises it makes, and the whole majestic presence of the animal. But I would say, now, that a wounded lion or leopard is far more dangerous.

'The average hunter goes through four distinct stages of experience. In the beginning he's nervous and apprehensive, even over-careful. Then he learns that in normal conditions, with the wind right, very great liberties can be taken. He takes them, with impunity, and tends to get rather reckless. That's the second stage. Then he either gets a packet by getting a mauling or a narrow escape from one, and learns to be intelligently careful. By now he's assessed the animal at its proper value, and acts accordingly. The fourth and last stage is when he's getting old, and thinks his reactions are still as quick as they were ten years before, which of course they're not. That's how a lot of old hunters get killed.

'The greatest fear, you know, is *before* and *after* the incident; at the actual charge one feels practically nothing. The early stages are the worst, before you've seen the animal, but you know he's aware of you and not far ahead. One follows up step by step, trying to make good every scrap of cover, every bush and branch. A bird gets up and you jump into the air; your hair feels like standing on end; you start to sweat. Then you have to be careful, for this is the stage of fear when you make mistakes. There's one important point, incidentally, that I've never seen mentioned in any book—I mean the importance of taking continual rest. Every moment of pause, whenever you can, you should relax and rest, even if it's only for a second, so that you don't become nervously exhausted. Carelessness on these occasions is entirely due to nervous exhaustion, in my opinion. It's such a strain, often very prolonged, momentarily expecting an unseen animal to charge from any direction, that when the charge actually comes the feeling is quite definitely one of relief. No, I'm sure it's true to say that one feels practically no fear at all when the animal charges. When it's all over, of course, that's a different matter. Trembling, lassitude, coldness, one can feel all those things. But everything has to be paid for, and without the fear you wouldn't have the excitement.'

The narrowest escape from death he has had was in 1932, when having recently left the army and spent several months illegally (and not very profitably) ivory-poaching in the Congo, he was trying to make a living out of elephant-hunting, this time legally, shooting for ivory on licence. (He had been seconded at his own request to the King's African Rifles with the sole motive of getting himself to Africa, where he could spend his leaves on the kind of hunting expeditions that he longed for, and where eventually, he hoped, he might be taken on by the Tanganyika Game Department. Now, though he had left the army, he had still not succeeded in getting the job he coveted, and was on his own in Tanganyika, short of money and living by his own devices.) He was nearly at the end of his current licence, which entitled him to one more elephant, and had set his heart on getting a hundred-pound pair of tusks, on the proceeds of which he could live for several months.

'I was hunting through very thick forest at the time, camping rough, with only an African guide and a couple of bearers. Time was short because money was running out; I needed only one elephant with warrantable tusks to fill up my licence, and was determined to get that hundred-pounder before I went much further. Well, on this particular morning we came across the spoor of a small breeding herd, cows and calves, and a little farther on the fresh spoor of two bull elephants, moving on their own. Presently the track of the cows went right across that of the bulls, from left to right, and I thought, "Thank God the cows and calves are out of the way, so that I can follow up the bulls and get a look at their tusks." After a little while, edging up very cautiously through the trees, I heard the sound of elephant not far ahead; I had very sharp hearing in those days, not like now. I took my rifle—we had only the one—and sent back my people a little way, as was my custom. Almost at once I heard the sound of a single shot, a muzzle-loader, and asked the guide if he thought there were any Africans in the vicinity who might be taking a crack at the elephant. He said he thought it improbable; we were near the edge of the forest, with open plain beyond, and he thought it likely that someone was taking a shot at a water-buck. This seemed a reasonable explanation, and I went on alone.

'Presently I came to a small clearing, about six paces across, and partly concealed in the bushes on the other side of it were my two elephants. The first was facing me, the whole of the head and forepart rising out of the scrub; of the other I could see only a patch of hide, and didn't know what part of the animal I was looking at. As I could see at once, the elephant facing me was bloody angry. (I discovered later, these were two of the cows, not bulls at all, and what had annoyed her was undoubtedly that shot.) She was standing with her ears and tail up, ominously swinging her head from side to side. The tusks, as I saw to my disappointment, were quite unwarrantable, so I ran a little way across the clearing to try and get a better view of the other animal.'

'Wasn't that rather unwise?'

'It was very foolish indeed, as were all my actions on this particular occasion. I was asking for it. The next thing I saw, out of the tail of my eye, was the first elephant coming purposefully towards me. I turned and fired a shot at the head—I was very cocky in those days and thought I could stop any elephant with a single shot. She came on without a pause, and before I could fire again she was very close indeed. It's usual, you know, for a charging elephant to come at you with the head lowered and the chin stretched out, tusks advancing close to the ground, like a cow-catcher. I had barely time to fire a shot at the face, with the animal still coming, and did the only thing possible—turned and made a flying dive for the bush. Of course the inevitable happened; I tripped my foot over a branch and fell flat on my face. I lay still, praying that she'd miss the target and wouldn't find me. There was an extraordinary pause. The next thing I knew was a crash of twigs all round and the tusks appeared a foot or so in front of my head, digging up the ground. Looking up I saw a grey chin hanging above me, and knew that I couldn't get away. This was a moment that ought to have inspired the maximum of fear, but I distinctly remember thinking, almost with detachment, "Now I shall never get that hundred-pounder that I was working so hard for." The next feeling was also quite dull and detached, as though all this were happening to somebody else. I thought, "I've been asking for this for quite a long time, and now it looks as though I've got it." It was an extraordinarily remote and impersonal feeling—certainly there was no acute fear.'

'Didn't Livingstone record almost the same sensation, when he was being mauled by a lion?'

'He did, exactly. During the mauling, he said, there was "no sense of pain nor feeling of terror"—and he had to have an artificial joint in his shoulder after the mauling. It could be a sort of euphoric condition, caused by some action of the adrenal gland, perhaps? I don't know. At least it's a very merciful provision of nature, and I believe quite general. I've talked to a number of people who've been through a mauling, and they all confirm it. Well anyway, there I was, thinking these detached thoughts and apparently not at all concerned with my situation.

'The next thing was that the tusks had disappeared and something very heavy came down between my shoulders and scraped me violently backwards along the ground. The pressure was heavy, so that I had difficulty in breathing, but even then I felt no acute pain. The next thing she did was to start kicking me about between her fore and hind feet; I can distinctly remember trying to roll out of the way, but with about the third blow I passed out and I've no idea what happened after that.

'When I came round I was lying on my face in a different part of the clearing, some distance from the spot where the elephant had caught me. I couldn't see out of one eye; I was in no pain but I felt deathly ill, and could still hear the elephant rumbling very near. There was nothing to do but to go on lying there, hoping that the elephant would call it a day and not bother any more about me. Their fits of temper are short, as a general rule. But I lay for an intolerably long time while nothing happened, and presently it seemed to me that the rumbling was farther off. I started to turn my head very slowly, moving it as imperceptibly, I hoped, as the hands of a clock, and at last I could see that the clearing was trampled and empty; the elephant had disappeared, though I could still hear her in the bushes at a little distance. I cautiously wiped my eye, which I thought was burst, and found it was not my blood but hers which had been blinding me. I shook my limbs one by one and found nothing broken, though my head felt funny; one of her feet had caught me a blow on the ear which I afterwards found had permanently damaged my hearing. I couldn't walk, but I could crawl; my feet were tangled up in my shorts, which had been pulled very nearly off; I soon got out of those, I can tell you. I managed to get into the bushes, and there my Africans—who were quite unarmed and very near, I take off my hat to them—gathered me up and supported me back to camp.

'It took a long time, and all that day and the next I felt frightfully ill. I was sick and faint, weighed down with lassitude, and now that it was all over I had spasms of sweating fear; it kept coming over me in waves. And then of course there were the nightmares. Very bad they were. Oh, shocking. But there it is; in this whole business the *real* pleasure, what one calls the excitement, is simply another name for, another phase of fear. Without the fear one wouldn't be able to enjoy it. Odd, isn't it?'

'Did you ever learn what happened to the elephant?'

'Oh yes. My rifle had been left in the clearing, and as it was the only one I had it had got to be retrieved. My gun-bearer had managed to borrow a rifle from somewhere, and as I couldn't go myself I sent him back next day to look for mine. Though nothing was broken I was black and blue and stiff as a board; oh yes, quite literally. When I wanted to sit up I had to be levered up in one piece, like a plank. Stiff as hell I was for days; couldn't walk. I gave my man strict instructions to be careful; if he so much as heard elephant he was to come straight back, and wait till the coast was clear. Well, he went off, and after a time I heard a single shot, and then silence. I suffered considerable anxiety, you can imagine; he might have been injured or killed, and there was I helpless, able to do nothing. But he came back in the evening all right, complete with my hat and rifle and the elephant's tusks. My first bullet, he'd found, had passed right through the head, and my second through the thick part of the trunk and below the brain. There was blood all over the shop, and she'd torn up the ground with her tusks in three places.'

If it was miraculous that he had escaped with his life on this occasion, it seemed to me scarcely less so that he had got away with no graver hurt than a damaged ear-drum and a lingering tendency to bad dreams. And the deafness is only partial; his hearing is suspiciously selective. He would hear the note of a bird or the rustle of a leaf, or the first far-off hum of a vehicle seconds before I did, and I had the impression that his occasional failure with the human voice was less a matter of deafness than convenience. On the edge of the ravine, where we would crouch talking until the muscles of my legs ached (as his, so much thinner and harder, never did) he rarely failed to catch the quietest word, for one of the charms of his conversation is that he is equally concentrated as talker and listener. He would hear the stealthy rustle of some small animal among the leaves, would be able to tell when Makanga, whom we had left chopping wood behind the house, had finished the day's supply, or when a bare-footed child on the level ground behind us (there had been an emergency air-strip once and the earth is hard) was leisurely coming our way with a handful of cattle. Whether this means that his deafness is less of a handicap than he pretends, and that he chooses his sounds, or that he hears by vibration through the bones of his skull like a snake, I have no idea. As I got to know him better I was inclined to accept the second alternative as the more characteristic, and therefore, though not conclusively so, the more probable.

VII

CONVERSATION AT NIGHT

GRADUALLY, as the days went by, the scattered jig-saw of Ionides' personality—no, more than his personality, the essence, history and whole logic of the man—began to come together in a pattern which I could recognize and love. I found, as something in me had prophesied when I had first encountered him two years before (a remote and arresting figure standing alone in the crowd on Waterloo Station, brown-skinned, white-haired, in the same thin khaki trousers and canvas sneakers that I now so regularly followed through the bush), that in spite of all our disparities of circumstance and nature—and they could hardly have been more extreme—we came together with surprising ease on a common ground of agreement and recognition. What that common ground precisely was, I have never been able to determine, but its atmosphere was mysteriously related to that of childhood and the sense one then had of the innocence of the world. I cannot come any nearer to it than that; I know only that after the first few hours, when we were a little wary and polite with one another, the barriers of strangeness melted away and it suddenly became possible to say anything. I have since, re-reading Bertrand Russell's *Portraits from Memory*, been struck with sudden delight and recognition by a passage in his account of his meeting with Conrad. 'In all this'—they had fallen at once into unembarrassed discourse—'I found myself closely in agreement with him.

At our very first meeting, we talked with continually increasing sympathy. We seemed to sink through layer after layer of what was superficial, till gradually both reached the central fire. It was an experience unlike any other that I have ever known. We looked into each other's eyes, half appalled and half-intoxicated to find ourselves together in such a region. The emotion was as intense as passionate love, and at the same time all-embracing. I came away bewildered, and hardly able to find my way among ordinary affairs.'

If I cannot pretend that our discussions were as profound as theirs, if they were often childish and full of unseemly laughter, the sense of agreement, of finding under our manifold differences areas which we constantly illumined for one another, was nevertheless moving, was warm and nourishing on its simple level. As the evenings grew colder and we waited for the moment when Makanga, having give us in turn our two bucketfuls of boiling water in the murky bath, would drag in a load of wood and light a fire which turned the vault-like living-room into an oven, we would both be conscious of a long forgotten eagerness for the dark hours, with the wind creaking and straining at the corrugated roof, the snakes in their boxes still or restless, the hurricane lamp on the table throwing barred shadows and everything conspiring to create a warm illusion of timeless intimacy. We soon developed a ritual which seemed the very essence of domestic comfort. Dismayed by the singular horror of Makanga's coffee, which Ionides drank every night without complaint, I had insisted on buying a tin of a brand known to me (the tin was small and quite useless for packing reptiles, but I noticed that Ionides afterwards frugally made use of it for butterflies) and encouraged Makanga before he went to bed to bring us two cups, diluted milk-powder, some sugar, and a kettle. As soon as we were alone and the doors locked (everything had to be locked because of thieves) I would boil the kettle, holding it at length on an iron poker because of the fierceness of the fire, and brew up a beverage which at home would have caused me to turn away with a shudder, but which then seemed the height of luxury to us both. The fire would grow hotter and hotter and we would retreat to our chairs at the farther side of the room, wedged in between the gramophone and the snakes. I occupied myself most evenings with hemming the edges of the cotton *kangas* I had bought in the village; the room was so close at night that the only comfortable thing to do was to wear them. Sometimes even Ionides would discard his pullover, performing a complicated sloughing manœuvre, since at this hour the jersey was concealed under a threadbare dressing-gown which, with mosquito boots pulled up over the legs of his trousers, was his evening costume; and this was my opportunity for carrying out a gradual programme of repairs, darning the holes with some brown wool which I later found, when I was reckless enough to wash the thing, was the wrong colour.

Occasionally, when our feelings seemed to warrant it, the coffee would be followed by glasses of gin and water. Ionides, to put it mildly, is an abstemious man, and when hunting has always been completely teetotal; but in congenial company he will drink a little wine or small quantities of gin, and there was always a bottle of spirits on the chimneypiece. It had to be kept there because there was nowhere else to put it; the fireplace was a huge affair of brick with a ledge running round the chimney on which calico bags for packing snakes were kept, the goggles we wore when dealing with spitting-cobra, the tongs, empty gin bottles used for drinking-water, and, of course, the gin. The chimney-breast reached such a high temperature in the course of the evening that it never entirely cooled during the day, and the contents of the bottles, even with a slice of lime to sharpen the stickiness, reminded me of those drinks one used to be given at the onset of a cold, under the guise of toddy. But we were not particular, and very little made us slightly hilarious. As Stanley so justly observed somewhere in the early pages of *How I Found Livingstone*, 'It requires somewhat above human effort, unaided by the ruby liquid that cheers, to be always suave and polite amid the dismalities of native life in Africa.' We were not always suave and polite, for Ionides' vein of pleasantry tends, though with the utmost gravity, to exaggeration. 'Shall we get bestially drunk tonight?' was his usual courtly preamble to gin and water.

I was puzzled, listening to his uninhibited talk and considering the extreme respectability of his family and upbringing, that he should refer to his Congo ivory-poaching, or to youthful adventures of pheasant-poaching and chicken-stealing, as though they were a regular part of middle-class experience, something that could happen to any young man or schoolboy of normal spirit. He admitted on reflection that perhaps it was, after all, a trifle unusual, and that he had always been strongly attracted to breaking the law. Why this should be so he could not say, unless it were that illegal pursuits, involving additional risk, yielded just that extra refinement of fear to an enterprise which made it thoroughly enjoyable. 'In different circumstances, I dare say, I might have been quite a distinguished juvenile delinquent. Poaching pheasants is exciting, you know. I did a certain amount of it in the holidays, and also at school. My parents never knew about it, naturally, though I think my father must have got an inkling after I'd gone into the army, and he came across a secret drawer with a lot of rabbit-nets in it, and things like that. And of course it all came out when I had to leave school; they found my sawed-off shotgun and various implements of poaching, and the head of a wild duck which I'd mounted on board. But my father never said anything explicit; I think he was fed up by this time with all the trouble there'd been, and didn't want to know more than was absolutely necessary.' (Ionides had finally left Rugby under a cloud, at the peak of a career of defiance and endurance which is still remembered; he had been beaten eighteen times his first term, thirteen his second, and after that lost count. Spare-time poaching had been the chief offence, but suspicion had also been expressed over a mysterious theft of money from a locker, of which he knew nothing. He was not expelled—even Rugby could hardly do that without evidence—but his father was asked to remove him, and very creditably, less out of sympathy than pride, refused; a moral stand for which his son is grateful. But not long after, family dignity assuaged by the delay, he in fact left school and was reasonably happy under the maturer system of freedom and discipline which he found at Sandhurst.)

'Certainly the poaching and the chicken-stealing—and there wasn't much of *that*, it only happened once or twice—had nothing to do with my environment, or being set a bad example by anyone else. Such associates as I had were always followers; I was the leader. I suppose you could say it was a streak of latent evil in my nature. I was always, even from a child, attracted to the idea of breaking the law, and fancied myself as a rather hearty type of villain. Captain Hook, you know—perhaps you might call him an influence?—I always thought him an attractive character. Then, as far as the poaching was concerned, it was just a natural love of hunting combined with the charm of illegal action, which carried an extra risk. Of course there would have been a frightful row if my father had known at the time, but he never did. The servants knew, but they jolly well kept their mouths shut. They were on my side; they loved it.'

He never went in for night poaching, and had only one momentary brush with a game-keeper who fortunately failed to recognize him and whom he easily knocked down (he had been a good boxer at Rugby); but in his enthusiasm for crime he had provided himself with an armoury which would certainly have got him into trouble if he had been caught with it. 'I had the stock and barrel, without the tail-piece, of a single-barrelled shotgun, which I got while I was still at Rugby—bought it at Cogswell and Harrison—and sawed it off to a short length with the blade of a hacksaw. To carry it I cut out the inside pocket of my jacket and elongated that right down to the bottom; this carried the stock. Then I sewed a ring into the arm-hole of my waistcoat which nicely carried the barrel, hooked into it. Then one had, of course, the large ordinary poacher's pockets into which one could put game, and I also used to put birds down the legs of my plus-fours. I remember one nasty moment when I was stopped for a chat by an unsuspecting policeman, and looking down saw the head of a pheasant dangling out of a hole in the knee of my plus-fours. He didn't notice it, fortunately. Then as well as these things, later on, I had a handy cosh or life-preserver, and eventually, I'm sorry to have to tell you, a knuckle-duster.'

'Did you ever use either of them?'

'Er . . . no. Looking back I can see it was fortunate I never did. Though there was one occasion during the school holidays, and another at Sandhurst, when I was eighteen, when I was prepared to use them, though luckily it didn't come off. The first was a chicken-stealing incident, in which I was involved with a friend. This friend of mine had recently been removed—or expelled, I don't remember which—from Eton, where he had a particular enemy, one of the house-masters. This fellow kept chickens as a hobby, and the theft was planned in revenge. I didn't join in this vendetta out of benevolence, you understand, but because it was enjoyable. I carried the cosh, I remember, but the operation went off quite smoothly, without incident, and I had no occasion to use it. The second was a more serious affair. I had a great friend at that time who'd recently left Lancing College.' ('Removed or expelled?') 'I don't remember. Anyhow, he knew that on a particular date at the end of term the journey-money for the boys was kept in a certain house-master's room, and we planned a burglary. He, knowing the way, would break into the room and take the money, while I waited outside with my cosh or life-preserver, to deal with anybody who interrupted us. The money would all be in small currency for the boys' fares, so we thought we should get away with that all right. God knows why we didn't realize what a stupidly dangerous thing we were embarking on; but anyhow, that was the scheme. I can see now that it was highly lucky for both of us that when the plan was on the point of fruition this friend of mine, driving at night on a fast Matchless motor-bicycle, crashed into a motor-car and broke his leg, so the whole thing fell through. But at the time one was very sorry.'

Even now, his attitude to the law is far from reverent. 'I've no exaggerated respect for it *as such*. I recognize the fact that you've got to have laws; most of them contribute to a perfectly sensible way of living together, and I observe them, I pay my taxes regularly and I look on petty law-breaking as silly. All the same, the mere fact that a thing was illegal wouldn't prevent me from doing it if I considered it was to my advantage to do so, and thought I could get away with it.'

Whether or not this attitude is contradictory in a man who himself exerts such natural authority, I am not sure. Probably not, any more than it is strange to find honour among thieves or discipline among bandits; one can imagine Ionides ruling with ferocious relish from headquarters in a mountain cave in Sicily. But it was not a point of view which endeared him to his superiors in the army, and though he found his six years of soldiering congenial enough, he lacked, he admits, the whole-hearted devotion to regulations and tradition which makes for promotion and the career of a successful officer. Army life, he found, was perfectly tolerable; it took him away from the cold, crowds, noise and boredom of urban England, and first in India and later in East Africa put him in reach of jungle and bush, where the wild life was a continuous enthralment and he could save up his pay and his leaves for the solitary intoxication of big-game hunting. Planning these expeditions and reading about other hunters' experiences occupied the chief of his attention; with much of army life he was frankly bored. 'I wasn't at all popular, and can see why. I never could join wholeheartedly in the worship of the horse, which was a very serious religion in those days, or in that other compulsory mystique of *loving one's men*. So much that went on struck me as a waste of time, and I suppose this was noticed.' Still, it was a shock when he got a thoroughly bad report in the K.A.R., which upset him until he had time to reflect that this was one of those apparent disasters in life which were really disguised benefits, since it precipitated his resolve to leave the army. 'The C.O.'s annual confidential report was usually stuffed with fulsome praise, especially under the heading "Zeal and energy. . . ." *Anything* critical, however slight, was taken very seriously. *My* zeal and energy, I'm sorry to say, came out as "below average", and this was followed, under "Remarks", by the nasty but possibly truthful observation that "It would be to his advantage, and to the advantage of the service, if he took as much interest in his profession as he does in big-game shooting." I don't think the colonel himself had anything against me; he was simply echoing his second-in-command's prejudice, which was partly due to my having annoyed his wife. However, there was great good in it, as one often finds when considering one's reverses, for it made up my mind to get out of the army as quickly as I could and try to get into the Tanganyika Game Department.'

In this he was at first unsuccessful ; the Chief Game Warden of the time had heard that he had private means ('Two hundred a year, it couldn't be called wealth') and concluded that he was a dilettante and therefore unsuitable. There was 'No opening'. Money was getting short; he was determined to stay on the spot in Africa until he could edge his way into the Game Department, and a spell of ivory-poaching in the Congo seemed a natural and profitable idea, combining business with pleasure. 'This was at the end of 1929, and it only lasted a few months. It wasn't nearly as profitable as I'd hoped, for I need hardly tell you that as soon as I took it up, the price of ivory, in the Congo and elsewhere, dropped dramatically.'

Ivory-poaching, which sounds like something out of an exotic cookery book, was a new idea to me, and had to be explained. The shooting of elephant, as of every other valuable large animal, is done on government licence, and licences everywhere cost a great deal of money. The ivory poacher is usually a man who operates secretly, without licence, working often close to the border between two countries, so that the tusks obtained in one can be transported with minimum risk and sold in the other. 'In those days there was no real stigma attached to poaching, you know; the only rule was, you mustn't be caught. One wasn't conscious, then, of the diminishing number of animals, and the thing was dangerous and illegal and had a certain glamour. In any case, the one animal I never worry about is the elephant. They go on breeding and increasing in spite of everything, and always have to be controlled. There wasn't so much anti-blood-sports talk in those days, and being a hunter, even outside the law, was pretty well regarded, provided that you were—I hope you'll excuse the expression—a sportsman.

'There's more than one method of elephant-poaching. The partner I worked with for a time used to cross into the Congo by night with two or three canoes, stay there hunting for a short while, and as soon as it got too hot for him would bung the ivory into the canoes and get it to a Tanganyika trader, who as likely as not would sell it back illicitly to the Congo. I worked on a different system. I went quite openly into the Congo and bought a licence; in each province you could get a licence to shoot two elephant a year. (A better technique, which I didn't think of at first, was to make my headquarters at the junction of three provinces and take out three *permis de chasse*, which I operated simultaneously; but in the beginning I had only one.) It was quite difficult to get, because of course the authorities knew quite well what one was after, and made a lot of difficulty. Anyhow, once you'd got it, the thing was to keep on for a long time shooting your first elephant, all the time smuggling the stuff away to an ivory buyer who was willing to break the law. One went on with the "first" elephant until it got to be pretty generally known what was going on, and then it was prudent to register a pair of tusks. Then I went on ostensibly shooting the second elephant, until the same problem arose. I had the co-operation of the natives, needless to say; they took it as a matter of course. Going on safari wasn't expensive, not the way I did it. I travelled with two porters, changing them frequently, and only two personal boys. There was a "white man's hut" in those days in every village, exceedingly comfortable you know, a roof and everything. Chickens were cheap, only a few pence; you could shoot a buffalo when you needed to, and that lasted a long time. I used to carry my money, all paper currency, in a bag round my neck, so that if I had to get out I could get out quickly. I always disposed of each pair of tusks as I got them, sending them off to the trader and getting the money back quickly, so that I always had my assets in portable form.

'The only way to sell the ivory was to pass it through the native chiefs, who had native-authority rights to shoot elephant with their own weapons, and it was therefore necessary for them to claim the elephant as theirs, and get the official permit to sell the ivory. They demanded their rake-off, naturally; I used to bribe them quite heavily. In the early days they hadn't demanded so much, but at this time they were beginning to get greedy, and each one was jealous of the others. If one chief thought another had got more than he had, he was liable to make a lot of trouble. But it usually worked out all right. I had to have six people ready to carry the ivory by night, hiding it during the day; the best way was under water. The following night it would be picked up by the next lot of people and carried to another *cache*, and so on, until finally it got to the trader and I got my money.'

By this time the fire would be burned to an incandescent heap, Ionides' face would be lit by the glow and the room thick with the smoke from his cigarettes. It was probably late, but we kept no account of time. The hours of the night were lovely in this private oven, incomparably better than the tedium of darkness and bed. Besides, once embarked on the techniques of ivory-poaching I was kept afloat and awake by the charm of useless and recondite information which I could never conceivably profit by and would never have thought myself in the least likely to possess.

'You haven't explained how you get the tusks out of an elephant?'

'Ah, that can be troublesome. In the normal way you chop them out with an axe. That requires some strength and skill, but at least it's quick. The risk is, however, that you may damage the ivory. The safer method is to wait till the animal has rotted down, and draw them out, but this takes time; about a week in the case of a big elephant. I didn't as a rule, when poaching, have time for this, so I used to build a hot fire on the elephant's forehead; this, you'll find, greatly accelerates the processes of rotting.'

'And the carcase, did you do anything with that?'

'I'm afraid the carcase usually had to be wasted, which was a pity. Elephant meat in the Congo fetched a lot of money, but if the meat was cut up and sold all over the area everyone in the place knew that an elephant had been killed, and this, as you will appreciate, was precisely what I didn't want. The natives near the spot knew it anyway, but they all owed obedience to the chief, who was receiving a bribe, so I made sure that he realized that if *I* got into trouble, *he*'d be in the next cell. They always wanted to sell the meat, of course, to make money, and the only certain way of preventing this was to burn the body of the elephant, which can be done by cutting down a large amount of firewood, piling it up and making a big bonfire. Oh yes, an elephant will burn. How long does it take? Oh, once it's well alight, you know, it's all right. I've never waited till it was absolutely reduced to ashes, the important thing was always to get away. And the light of the fire didn't show up very far; the uplands were covered with high grass and the rivers thickly forested, and the elephant were always killed in the forested valleys. I don't recollect many vultures, not enough, at least, to give the show away. The problem didn't arise in that part of the Congo; it wasn't a worry, like the Belgian authorities, who were always spying. But unfortunately they were a pretty corrupt lot; their attention was easily distracted with a bit of offal. Financial offal, of course.'

Nevertheless, in spite of his own precautions and the venality of petty officials, a *procès verbal* was made out against him on one occasion which led to his appearing in court. 'But it turned out satisfactorily. I bribed all the witnesses; they spoke such poor Swahili that I even had to coach them in court. So what with one thing and another the evidence was so hopelessly conflicting that the case had to be dismissed.' It had been in fact a case of blackmail, the result of financial jealousy between two chiefs. 'I'd shot an elephant on the land of a chief with whom I'd already bargained, but it fell on the land of another with whom I'd not made any arrangement. Some time after this, when the tusks had been disposed of, I got a blackmailing letter from the second chief, demanding half the value of the tusks, or he would report me to the D.C. I dealt with this by sending a letter to the chief who was my accomplice, informing him that if I went to prison I'd see that he went there too, so it was up to him to help me. I instructed him that the only evidence was the remains of the elephant, which by this time were merely bones, lying about just outside his boundary. I told him to send his young men over at night to remove every bone and transport them to his own territory, which he did, and this fortunately closed the incident, for what with the bribed witnesses and the absence of bones, the case really faded away for want of evidence.'

The only other brush with the law had been some years later, when in the course of a perfectly legal hunting expedition into the Congo (this was when he had started rarity-hunting and was after an okapi) he had done a little experimental snake-catching, and had sent off a parcel of live specimens to a Port Elizabeth museum.

'The Customs started poking about with the parcel, and found a live Jackson's tree-snake, a ditto black-and-white cobra and two horned vipers. There was quite a lot of trouble about that, and another *procès verbal*. "Il est totalement interdit d'envoyer les serpents vivants . . ." and so on.'

'But was it really illegal to send live snakes anywhere?'

'Certainly it was, by ordinary post.'

'By *post* . . . ?'

'Oh yes; this was early days, you know, I hadn't got the thing organized. I sent the first lots in ordinary gunny-bags, and on one unfortunate occasion the bags weren't properly sewn up, and arrived empty. I've often wondered what happened to those cobras.'

When finally, after a further three years of making an erratic (but perfectly legal) living out of ivory and as a White Hunter, he was taken on by the Tanganyika Game Department, he felt no more embarrassment in pursuing other law-breakers than I imagine is usually felt by any poacher turned gamekeeper. He knew the tricks of the trade, and found his knowledge invaluable on the other side of the fence. Stalking poachers was in its way as absorbing as following elephant; a good practitioner was a worthy opponent; the only change was that he now found himself on the side of the law, and—a position infinitely more congenial—on the side of the elephant. He looks back on his ivory-poaching with mixed feelings, for even in the early days the haste and waste of the thing were antipathetic. 'As a boy I never wasted anything I killed. I can't remember ever shooting an animal just for the hell of it and leaving it on the ground. Even the mice I used to catch at prep-school I always skinned. I used to treasure the skins and skeletons, and was called "a disgusting little brute" for keeping them in my desk. But that was all part of the charm, you see, a combination of hunter's and collector's lust, which I had from the beginning. The complaint at school was always "Doesn't concentrate"—but the trouble was, I *over*-concentrated; only it wasn't on school subjects, it was on wild animals. When I was sixteen I went to a taxidermist and paid him to give me a lesson in skinning and stuffing a bird. I've never been very good at it, being rather ham-handed, but at least it gave me the satisfaction of being able to preserve my specimens, which is an important step if you're eventually going to turn into a naturalist.'

The change that came over him in this respect after his ivory-poaching days is very marked, but he cannot remember when it was that the wastage involved began seriously to oppress him. 'It's difficult to say. I suspect, when it's a question of a gradual change in one's own behaviour, one begins by disapproving of other people, and after a time, by a logical process, one turns the disapproval on oneself. I'm trying to think whether, if I were not lame and were still able to do it, it would give me any pleasure *now* to shoot an elephant. Only, I think, in very special circumstances. If it was a very rare animal . . . that's to say, if it was an enormous tusker required by a museum . . . if the difficulty of getting it was *very* great, and I knew that the whole animal would be used, that it would be skinned and mounted . . . then, yes, I think I would. But just to shoot the beast and dispose of the ivory, no, definitely not; not in the very least. I passed out of that phase years ago. If you go on doing things just for the thrill of it they go bad on you later. Don't we get more exacting as we grow older? That's where the naturalist's interest comes in; the killer turns preserver. Those hunters who never outgrow the first stage have simply failed to grow up, in my opinion.'

The first symptom of change in his attitude was a passionate interest in the idea of rarity-hunting. This was partly endemic, an idea which had always held a strong attraction, but was precipitated by his picking up a book called *Big Game Hunting in Africa* by H. C. Maydon, which stressed the importance and fascination of rarity-hunting and greatly influenced him. It channelled his ambitions in the direction of a new obsession, and set him on a course which was to bring him the keenest experiences of his life. 'I don't know how other people feel at my time of life, but it seems to me that I've achieved far more than I ever dreamed was possible when I was a young man. By achievement I mean, defining one's objective and consciously attaining it. I perhaps didn't set my sights very high by some people's standards, but I knew what I wanted, and on a satisfying number of occasions I succeeded in getting it. The thing becomes an obsession, you know, this rarity-hunting. You can't think of anything for weeks and months on end other than the addax or okapi or whatever it is you're after, and when you get it, after months of hard work—my God, the reaction! You're trembling and weak, you can't get to sleep at night for the shock of realizing you've actually done it—oh, there's nothing like it! Until, of course, the next one comes along. . . .'

He learned much during these expeditions, for which he saved his money for years at a time and on which he spent all his leaves from the Game Department. The chief virtue he acquired (an essential one for a hunter, the only one, indeed, that he claims to possess) was patience; disappointment never discouraged him, but fed a manic persistence, so that he returned again and again to the pursuit of some elusive rarity, never relaxing mentally until he had achieved it. Part of the attraction, being the man he is, was the hardship involved; nothing attracts him that can be gained without difficulty. Food on these expeditions, travelling on foot and living off the country, was a problem which his natural asceticism easily solved; and here, as I listened to his account of the sustaining properties of things I would hardly have thought edible, I began to perceive the origins of some of his habits, and to understand even that solitary sausage, shrivelled and small as a dismembered finger, which was dissected longitudinally each day at breakfast, spread carefully with very old mustard from a plastic egg-cup, and consumed slowly. Compared with past breakfasts this was a civilized delicacy, and I could see why he respected it. On one well-remembered trip he had lived wholly on cassava root for five months, with an occasional stringy chicken, his only light a saucer of ground-nut oil with a scrap of shirt in it. On another, travelling by camel through the Sudan desert, he lived for a fortnight on a single ostrich egg, scrambling a little each day and plugging the hole with rag. And at other times he has eaten, with critical interest, monitor lizard and gaboon viper (he once, having nothing better, roasted a damaged gaboon viper for his Christmas dinner) and would no doubt, like Fabre, have explored the edible possibilities of grubs if there had been no alternative. Monitor lizard in fact (a huge and handsome reptile which I was later to see on the island of Mafia, trotting across the road like a high-stepping dragon) has, varied every now and then by trumpeter-hornbill, sustained him at home for considerable periods. I have no idea of the weight of a monitor lizard, but a fair specimen lasted him eighteen days. Majingililo has a special way with it, roasting it whole, taking the meat off the bones and pouring the melted fat over it—'making, in fact, a sort of primitive pemmican.' It reaches its peak of delicacy by the fifth day, when it is thoroughly gamey. (Ionides prefers his meat in this condition, easily arrived at in Africa; he regards refrigerators and all such unnatural devices with contempt.) After the seventh or eighth day, now in a more advanced stage, it becomes progressively tasteless, and in the third week even he will admit that it has little to recommend it. But his favourite bush food, when birds are unobtainable, is cane rat, and in describing its succulence his face lights up and his voice takes on the plummy tones of the gourmet. It is roasted, apparently, with the crackling on, and can without exaggeration be described as 'porcupine *de luxe*'—a comparison which would not have carried me very far without the tremor in his voice and the nostalgic expression.

Water on these expeditions is an even more serious problem than food, for in dry seasons the rarity must be shot before the water-bags give out, and enough kept in reserve for the return journey. Ionides prides himself on his resistance to hunger and thirst; carnivora, he likes to point out, can go without food for long periods without their strength being in any way impaired, and lions fast easily for eight days or even a fortnight. With such an example before him he would consider it shameful to be over-anxious about food, and has been pleased to find on the few occasions when he has followed an animal on foot for three days without food that a marked increase in fatigue on the last day was the only humiliating symptom. In the early years of his rarity-hunting he used always to practise deliberate austerities in the matter of eating and drinking, and a genuine indifference to both has become a habit; it is one of his mild vanities, another of those cherished freedoms by which he sets such store, and which has stood him in good stead in his stoic life. He is never aware if a meal is early or late, even fails to remark if he misses one altogether; an enviable state of affairs in a 'bush bachelor's' household; particularly fortunate, I could not help thinking, at Newala.

VIII

COBRAS AND OTHERS

IN all this time, though the house at the end of each week was crowded with snakes, I had not seen either a cobra or a python. This was strange, for while the black-and-white cobra is a sufficient prize for news of one to be worth twenty shillings, the spitting-cobra is common in the area, and pythons, at least in the steamy fringes of the Ruvuma, are not rare. But they were both coy, and we began to feel mildly annoyed at finding neither. Ionides does not normally collect pythons, which are constrictors and non-venomous and therefore of no interest to the venom-research centres among his customers. Besides, they are long-lived; a python supplied to a zoo will thrive for years, so that the demand is small. But spitting-cobras are always wanted, not only for the making of serum against snake-bite but also in cancer research, venom having been tried with some success as a pain-killer, and one or two are normally dispatched each week to laboratories in America.

Ionides has a special feeling for the cobra, which is brave, handsome and dangerous, the only snake in his experience which, unprovoked, seems occasionally in the mood for aggressive action. His favourites are the noble Indian cobra, the hamadryad, a creature of impressive size and beauty, and the black-and-white cobra, a fierce snake difficult to find, and therefore doubly desirable. But he does not despise the spitting-cobras of Tanganyika, which spray venom at the eyes of an enemy not near enough to bite, and which were responsible for no fewer than three local deaths during my stay at Newala. They are nocturnal snakes, hiding in banks and rat-holes during the day, where they can be reached only by long and patient digging; in the open they travel fairly fast and will rear and spread their hood ready for battle the moment they believe themselves to be cornered.

Lame though he is, and by habit extremely deliberate in his movements, when it suits him Ionides can show a turn of speed truly astonishing. I had sudden proof of this one afternoon when we were setting out for our stroll to the ravine, and in crossing a grassy patch behind the house, in the full flow of conversation, he caught sight of some movement quite invisible to me, and launched himself violently forward through the air, landing face downwards on the ground with arms outstretched, like a rugger player embracing an opponent's ankles. But the snake—it was a long, thin, stripe-bellied sand-snake that he had caught sight of—was even faster, and flashed away under an old scrap-heap, abandoned tractor parts and derelict boilers which the previous owner of the house had left behind. We spent a long time poking round this unpleasant pile, lifting old mud-guards and peering under broken wheels and back-axles, without success; the stuff was too heavy to lift, and the snake was as safe as if it had gone to ground in the Great Pyramid. The following day, still wandering about in the compound near the servants' quarters, he performed another feat of observation and speed, pausing to point to a twig on a tangled bush, and then, before I had time to distinguish the slender stem for what it was, making a pounce and drawing out a five-foot vine-snake, held by the neck. I was not allowed to touch this snake, for it is active and highly poisonous; a friend of his was once killed by one, and he has not forgotten it. 'Though it was his own fault really,' he said, holding up the narrow head between finger and thumb and looking intently in its face, his other hand casually gathering the lively coils; 'he was a Game Ranger who got interested in snakes and started trying to catch a seven-foot cobra, so I showed him how. He got quite good at it, and after a skinful was inclined to show off to his friends; so one day when slightly tight, of course, he got bitten. He didn't think much of it at first, there weren't any symptoms to speak of. Next morning he had a hangover; that was perfectly normal. Then he was sick; that was normal too. Then he started vomiting blood, which rather surprised him, and in forty-eight hours he was dead.' We walked thoughtfully back to the house, Ionides carrying the snake like a black skipping-rope, and it was put into a calico bag from which, at odd moments on the veranda steps when there was nothing to do, he liked to extract it cautiously for another look, showing me the clear pale eyes and distinctive markings. It was a nicely made snake, about the size of our tame *kisanga* and more fancily decorated; but its head was narrow and pointed, with a snout like a crocodile's, and I did not care for its expression.

The first cobra, so long awaited, was reported by Rashidi one night when we were sitting as usual by a roasting fire, enjoying the heat and the fumes of our private coffee. There was a soft step on the veranda and the wire screen of the inner door was pushed open. Only the one word, '*lipetera*', was spoken, but this means cobra, and before I had put down my cup Ionides had grabbed a torch and goggles from the chimney-piece and a forked stick from the floor, and had whisked out muttering into the darkness, the tails of his dressing-gown flying. I followed at once, running to catch up, but even at a trot it was difficult to keep pace with him. The moon was in its last quarter, but a mass of cloud was moving across the sky, and Rashidi's black legs and the dark dressing-gown were difficult to follow. I was wearing my *kanga*, too, which did not make things easier, for while the half of it which served as a shawl could be clutched with both hands, the other, normally secured (if that is the word) by tucking in the rolled edge under the armpit, develops troubles from which not even habitual wearers are immune, and I was in constant difficulty. However, I reached the place at last, an open patch of ground in front of one of the huts, where Rashidi was holding the feeble electric torch and Ionides, masked with goggles, was dodging about for a favourable position. The snake had been surprised in a corner, coiled in the dark behind a water-pot, and was now rippling smoothly along the base of the wall, black itself as the darkness and hard to see, intent only on escape. How it had been noticed in the first place I cannot imagine, nor how Ionides, guided only by the exhausted torch which was as good as useless, could follow its flowing speed and pin it to the ground; but in a few seconds he made a thrust with his stick and the long black body was casting about in the sand, applauded by the squeals and laughter of the onlookers. I had stood cautiously at the back of the group, having no goggles and not being sure how far it might spit its venom; and was glad, when a soft warmth on my feet told me that my *kanga* had fallen off entirely, that I was beyond the range of anyone's attention. I need not have worried about the venom, for during a cobra-catching a stream of Swahili from Ionides keeps everyone at bay, or at least more than ten feet away from the snake, that being its limit. This cobra was more frightened than angry, and made no attempt, at least that night, to retaliate; it neither reared nor spread its hood—'She bowed her head, she sheathed her tongue, And shining stole away'—and when the calico bag was produced went into it at speed and without protest, as though thankful to escape at last into peace and privacy.

Next day we took a closer look, for Ionides was anxious to show the snake in action, and to demonstrate a method, common among Indians who catch cobras professionally for snake-charming, of picking it up by the tail, a feat which requires some skill if one is not to get bitten. We took our cobra with us in the afternoon in the direction of the ravine, and released it on a patch of hard-baked sand where there was no cover and where we were fairly safe from the nuisance of onlookers. It rippled away from us as soon as it was free, undulating with a sideways motion which carried it over the ground with surprising speed; but the speed was only relative, no faster than the normal pace of a walking man, and Ionides headed it off each time with his forked stick, turning it again and again in another direction. It traversed the ground in this manner many times, leaving a wavy track behind it, crossing and re-crossing its path with dogged persistence. Only when Ionides tied his handkerchief to the end of the stick and fluttered it under the creature's nose did it rear and spread, flickering its tongue and staring with steady eyes at the apparition; but it neither struck nor spat, as though undeceived by these puerile pretences.

The 'tailing' of the cobra I could quite see, when this was performed, was a highly skilful measure, but the effect was alarming and undignified and I did not care for it. Ionides darted swiftly after the snake, caught it by the tip of the tail and held it at arm's length, shaking it up and down with a bouncing motion to distract its attention from his body and legs. It could have got him easily if it had had its wits about it, but all it did was to try to rear up its length to attack his hand, which it did repeatedly. Both I and the snake had had enough by this time, and I was glad when the display was over.

I concluded, mistakenly, that this was a patient snake, and conceived the idea of taking an impressive photograph. Cobras are often found lurking round native huts, their chief diet being rats; this one, I remembered, had been hiding behind a water-pot almost at Rashidi's door, and in my mind's eye I saw a pleasing picture of the cobra gliding out of the mouth of the vessel, never doubting that between us we would manage it. To my surprise

Ionides said it was impracticable, the cobra being unlikely to co-operate. However, he would try, and when we got home I went indoors for my camera. Then followed a performance of such skill, on the snake's part, that it would have been wonderful if it had not been so exasperating. First the cobra, held in the tongs, was lowered tail-first into the belly of the pot, and instantly sprang out vertically into the air, as though it had been fired from a catapult. Captured again without much difficulty it was now put in head-first, and disappeared completely. We waited, both wearing our goggles and I with my camera, and through an interminable and anxious wait nothing happened. My legs (we were both crouching) began to ache, and Ionides observed in a detached voice that cobras have been known to stay in pots for days, even when there was water in them. This began to look like being unprofitable, and the cobra could not be left there with any safety. Could we not, I asked, roll the jar partly over on its round bottom, so that the snake would be bound to emerge and I would get my picture? This was done carefully, though with some scepticism, with the forked stick; but African water-pots, being indeed round-bottomed, will gyrate in any direction but the one intended, and this one rolled with the mouth away from us, and the snake was gone in a flash. We made several more attempts, Ionides' patience wearing as thin as the cobra's, but by this time the snake was on to the game and was more than our match. It either lay, coiled and invisible in the depths of the jar, or sprang back again like a boomerang as soon as it was put into it, or else deceived the eye in some other unpredictable manner so that at the moment when my face was pressed to the view-finder it would be sprinting across the sand out of focal distance. At last we gave it up, and the snake was returned in triumph to its bag. I did get a series of photographs, none of them, sad to say, of the smallest interest. Several studies of pots, both upright and prone, with not a snake in sight; one, the best, of the water-pot upright with the tip of a black tail lying negligently over the lip; several of Ionides' hands and stick, and a close-up of Rashidi's sandals. I thought at the time that the difficulty was partly the goggles, which I was forbidden to remove, and that I might have done better without them. But I now know, having watched Ionides at work with other cobras, that he was perfectly right, and that photographing the spitting variety, with the snake moving freely and at close quarters, is not a job for novices.

Not long after this we tried, and failed, to dig out another cobra from a bank. (When I say 'we' I do not mean that I took any part in the digging, which was done with great energy by Pétu and Rashidi, nor that I ever handled a cobra beyond releasing the body from the grabs when I was told; my part was always that of a spectator.) It was an unlucky morning, for we had driven a good many miles on the report of a particularly large puff-adder, and when we reached the spot found that a trench had been dug round the snake and a heavy basket put over it. Ionides stopped short at this and turned at once on his heel, his face like thunder, muttering only as we clambered back into the Land Rover, 'Sweet little chaps! I'm only waiting for the day when one of them gets bitten and dies. It's bound to happen sooner or later.' We bumped our way back through the millet fields without speaking, coming at last to a narrow gully near the Makonde Water Works, a sunken lane overhung by tangled hedges. It was a much used path, and in the steep bank among tree-roots someone had seen, or claimed to have seen, a black-and-white cobra. There were certainly rat-holes here, a ramified warren, and the two boys, goggled like ourselves, began to chop carefully at the surface with their mattocks, uncovering hole after hole and testing the direction with sticks for the main burrow. It was very hot; even standing and waiting the sweat gathered under our goggles and ran down our faces. Women with water-pots, wearing the little black lip-plug of the Makua, came by at a stately pace and stayed to watch; men and boys, crop-headed girls and children stole up the path and banks to join the gathering, and soon the lane was so full of people, gaping and peering, that only a snake of prodigious size would have been a fitting climax. But no snake appeared, and after an hour or more Ionides, who had been squatting on his hams with a look of patient endurance, goggles pushed up on his sweating forehead, smoking incessantly and strewing the earth around him with spent matches, announced in a hollow voice that digging a cobra often took several days, and that when no snake was there, as he now suspected, the effort was perhaps not wholly worth it. The effort had been chiefly Pétu's and Rashidi's; they were taking it in turns, shining with sweat and evidently getting tired, but they were used to the work and would have gone on indefinitely if Ionides had not come to the conclusion that the wished-for cobra had never been seen at all, or at least not lately. The messenger was questioned, and came out of the interrogation badly. The cobra had been seen that morning. It had been seen yesterday. It was the biggest snake ever beheld in the neighbourhood. It had gone into that hole (pointing), or perhaps into that one; or perhaps it had surely gone in this other direction? It too often happens that a snake is reported that has never been seen at all, for where there are rat-holes there may be a black-and-white cobra; it is worth trying; the spirits of one's ancestors are powerful and the right kind of snake is worth twenty shillings. The atmosphere of equivocation was strong, and we were suddenly scattering the crowd and in motion again, disapprovingly shaking the dust of the place from our feet. It was some comfort that our last call that day produced a boomslang, a beautiful dark green snake which I had not seen before, though they are common enough. They mostly are of varying shades of brown, though some of them are black; this one was green and not much darker than a mamba, each scale outlined with a hair-fine border of black, the belly daffodil-yellow. It was taken without great trouble from a low thorn-tree and seemed unafraid, even when brought to the ground, making no attempt to strike when Ionides approached it, but turning and regarding him dispassionately with a yellow-green eye.

The second cobra-dig was three days later; a big snake was reported in the bank at the edge of the road by the mission hospital. This was conveniently near home; the school and hospital, staffed and run by a handful of Anglican nuns, is about as far on one side of Newala as Ionides is on the other. I had been there already once or twice, alone, and had been offered cocoa and biscuits by the sisters. Ionides disapproves of missionaries in general and had taken no interest in these visits. Now as the digging began and a crowd gathered I could see Sister Gloria, head nursing-sister and midwife, standing with a group of young women with babies on the higher ground, while a mixed throng of patients and their relations, some on sticks, some in bandages, some of them lepers, came hurrying over the grass for a better view. Considered as entertainment this was a full house, and I hoped the show would not end in disappointment, for while Ionides feigns to dislike a crowd he is less indifferent to its effect than he pretends. To have a defeat with such a public cobra (the first, of course, would have been already reported) would surely destroy his morning.

It began badly. The bank was thick with roots, a catacomb of rat-holes, galleries running off in all directions. First one tool was tried and then another, roots were chopped through, earth crumbled and fell, obscuring the direction, and it looked for a time as though the whole bank would be fruitlessly demolished. We even, after an hour of labour and suspense, gave the thing up and returned to the house in disgust, the memory of the earlier hoax still strong upon us. But the snake was there. By the time we had eaten and were discussing the inexplicable scarcity of cobras a boy came running into the compound, and in less than a minute we were on the road again, whirling away to the hospital in a cloud of dust.

The digging was resumed with increased caution. The tail of the snake had been momentarily seen, drawing itself out of sight into a deeper recess of the half-demolished passages, and it seemed that it was indeed a big one, as the messenger had said. No one could tell how far the warren extended, and it was as important to avoid injuring the snake as it was to prevent its escape from a further hole, where it might emerge in desperation among the onlookers. After a time it was plain we were getting closer, for more than once, as we peered through our goggles into a dark hole, a surge of something black withdrew at the end of it. Now the crowd was driven off, and Ionides and Rashidi were standing poised while Pétu dug on alone. And at last a coil of snake bulged out from a fall of earth, struggled with a convulsive effort to withdraw, and was caught in the grab. Little by little the earth was chiselled away, for the cobra was long and powerful and determined to drag its enemy down if it could; but its struggle was hopeless. Soon another coil appeared and was made fast, and the whole snake was pulled out by degrees, yard after yard it seemed, taut and resisting, and brought through the scattering crowd to the edge of the road.

This one was magnificently at bay, rearing up as far as it could from the thing that held it, hood spread wide like the hunching of polished shoulders, turning this way and that with narrow gaze, waiting for the moment to strike with its own weapons. Ionides motioned me closer and we admired it, ignoring the squeals and comments of the audience, who as usual regarded the snake as an object of mirth. I had not imagined that the underside of the hood would be so beautiful, or reveal such polished cleanness and delicacy of colour, for the dorsal scales were dusty black and it had just been dragged from a rat-hole in dirt and ignominy. But the muzzle and throat, I saw, were pale as ivory, and the spread hood, making the high-shouldered outline of a sitting hawk, was marked with moth-like patches of black, flushed with a tint which varied from cream to rose. The face was startlingly bird-like, accipitrine, flat-headed, the eye as deeply bright as polished jet. The whole hood and upper part turned, just perceptibly, as we moved, holding a perfect line, measuring the distance with its snake's accuracy, choosing the moment to strike. When we moved closer, still out of reach of its fangs, it suddenly spat. There was an instantaneous recoil and throw of the head, a glimpse of a pink mouth open to the gullet, and I found the legs of my trousers wet with venom. It spat again as Ionides approached; there were drops of moisture like quicksilver on the sand. Now, seeing the forked stick so close, and knowing, perhaps, that its venom was half spent, it turned in rage on the grab, attacking with open jaws and dripping fangs, curving its neck and striking repeatedly downwards, the action of a sea-bird breaking a shell on a stone. It was a last resource and useless, for the grabs held and the forked stick was in place, pressing the black and ivory neck in the dust while Rashidi proffered the tongs and calico bag. All was completed with brisk efficiency, the cobra kicking inside the bag until the wooden box was closed and nailed fast. The record was entered in Ionides' book and the sum of two shillings—two shillings for that princely cobra!—passed to the hand of the man who had first seen it. It was not a black-and-white cobra after all, but only one of the common or spitting variety, destined not for a heated cell in some European zoo but for the far-off swarming snake-pits of Miami.

It is strange to think that the venom from this same snake, milked from the fangs at intervals during its captivity, may be used in the making of serum which will eventually find its way back to the Newala hospital. All bush hospitals keep supplies of serum, which is usually effective when injected immediately. Deaths from snake-bite occur when people are bitten in places far from any medical outpost, and the remedy, if they reach it alive, is too late. (The three deaths recorded while I was at Newala were all of village Africans who, following a grassy path at night, unluckily trod too near a hidden snake.) There is also, as an additional risk, the reluctance of many Africans to go to hospital at all; they suffer acutely from the loss of freedom, from the chilling separation from family and friends, falling often into an apathy which has an effect as deadly as disease.

For this reason among others (the chief being poverty), bush hospitals run by missionaries are free and easy, unfastidious affairs. The hospital buildings at Newala are long, bare, airy mud-and-wattle huts, whitewashed and roofed with corrugated iron, where the mothers who can be induced to do so come for pre-natal examination, for the actual birth if the midwife anticipates difficulty, and to the baby clinic afterwards. Some of the huts are wards, where the patients, motionless bodies wrapped in their coloured *kangas* or a thin blanket, lie on wooden beds in a timeless trance of boredom, coming to life only when their relations, who sit outside and prepare food on the veranda, bring them a bowl of millet or a mess of beans. The hospital cannot afford to feed them, and in any case they would rather starve than eat what they are not used to, which may seem strange in a country where one of the greatest problems is malnutrition, but is a fact to be reckoned with. The nursing sisters themselves have little enough to live on and subsist chiefly on cassava, boiled to a mush and disguised in different ways; the stuff is grown as a 'famine crop' all over the area, and gives a sensation of fullness, being almost pure starch; but it contains little nourishment. Once it had been pointed out to me I could recognize the grey, dusty appearance of the skin, so different from Makanga's or Makabui's glossy black, which distinguishes a child suffering from malnutrition, and also, at this hungry time of year before the harvest, the gingery bloom on the hair which is another symptom. Malnutrition is responsible for many of the difficult births which the nuns preside over, for the mothers are often slenderly built, with small bones and narrow pelvises. Contrary to popular belief, African women do not necessarily give birth easily. The proportion of Caesarean births at Newala is surprisingly high, in spite of the average weight of an African baby at birth being only five pounds, as opposed to the six or seven pounds average for a European. The Indian women who come to the hospital (there is quite a little population of Indians at Newala, mostly Gujerati traders and small shop-keepers who seem to have no earthly contact or interest outside their business and stroll aimlessly about the village in the evenings, the ladies draped in black saris), have a much easier time in childbirth than the Africans, and make proportionately more fuss; they are said to be troublesome patients. Among the Makonde it is bad form to complain or cry out during labour, and the sisters are often touched by their endurance.

The babies I saw at the hospital, apart from those brought to the weekly clinic by their mothers (and how richly beautiful these young women looked, squatting or sitting on the ground in their clean bright *kangas*, one raspberry-pink, one crimson and black, one lemon and green, a string of bright beads round every neck and sometimes a gold ornament in a nostril) were of two sorts, malnutrition cases and motherless babies. One little wizened creature, a face so shrunken it might already have been mummified, legs as frail as the shanks of a starveling bird, was offered to me by Sister Gloria on one palm; when I took it in my hands it was difficult to believe that any regimen of care could make it human. The mother, a girl with empty-looking pendulous breasts, looked on impassively while we handled it, and when we returned it gave it without a glance to her own mother, who stifled its cries by stuffing her own leathery nipple into its mouth.

Other shrivelled babies were in other cots, awake and apathetic; from each, among coloured wrappings, looked up the same disconcerting agate eyes. Some of them had been prematurely born, and in a corner two mothers, serious sturdy-looking young creatures, were sitting with bent heads, milking their large soft breasts into enamel mugs. The babies, it seemed, were still too weak to suck. Bottle-feeding is not practicable in native villages; the babies usually die of some infection, and until they can suck must be kept in hospital and fed from a pipette. Babies whose mothers have died in childbirth are also kept until they can walk and feed, when they are returned to their relations. A bouquet of these, plump and lively, the delight of the African girls who were training as nurses, were playing in a bare room at the end of the ward. They were merry and thriving, and it was plain to see that this salvage of life, carried on with loving patience in harsh conditions, is one of the human rewards of the sisters' lives. Those lives are hard enough in all conscience, and their future, like that of all Europeans in Tanganyika, seems now uncertain; but it would not be easy to find a more serene or certain-seeming group of women.

This is understandable; working with birth and with children is so fertile an occupation, so satisfying and rewarding emotionally that the rigours of missionary life, the isolation, the poor food and fatigue, the insidious languors of the climate, are forgotten in the consciousness that life at its most innocent level is being served. But the long love-affair with leprosy, mainspring of so many missionary lives, is more mysterious, and to the outsider less easily explained.

There was a time, not many years ago, when leprosy was so nearly incurable as to make its victims outcasts from any society and therefore particularly attractive to the spirit that longed for dramatic and irrevocable self-sacrifice. This is so no longer; the new sulphone group of drugs has revolutionized the treatment of leprosy, so that the disease is, if not always capable of cure, at least controllable. This lifts the leper out of his old pit as a human reject, whom it was meritorious, because so difficult, to love, and puts him on a level with sufferers from other tropical diseases such as elephantiasis, which is just as horrifying in its extreme stages, but has none of leprosy's romantic-sacrificial connotations. If leprosy were to be wiped out there would be many dedicated men and women in the world, professed religious for the most part, who would feel strangely at loss. (Graham Greene recorded in one of his African journals that some of the nuns in the Congo seemed almost to resent the increasing number of cures—'It's a terrible thing, there are no lepers left here.') But this desirable state of affairs is still far off, and there are many tropical countries where leprosy remains a disheartening problem. It is a slow disease, taking sometimes as long as twenty years to manifest, by which time, though the disease may be arrested, the leper is often beyond effective help. In the southern region of Tanganyika there are many lepers, their numbers increased by those who come over the border from Mozambique, from areas where there is apparently no treatment; by the time they reach the out-patient clinics of Newala or Lulindi they are often far gone in the disease and have left a secret trail of infection behind them. (A child at the breast, strangely, seems to be immune, though its mother may easily infect it after weaning; the disease is spread among Africans chiefly through the habit of using the same beds for long periods and wearing each other's clothes.) Again, fear of confessing to the disease and being confined, perhaps for years, to a leper hospital is one of the dreads which make wholesale treatment impossible; the preferred system among bush Africans, following the natural instinct for separation that divides the sound from the diseased, is to confine the sick man or woman to a hut at some little distance from the village, providing food until the sufferer dies. There is something to be said for this harsh method, for infection is not easily carried where there is no prolonged contact; but by the time the wretched leper has been cast out, perhaps after years in a crowded hut with his family, the damage is usually done.

Those who come to the clinics, even the highly infectious cases living there permanently, working as orderlies and dressers, are not always easily recognizable as lepers. The tell-tale coppery patches are not noticeable on a black skin, nor the slight puckering of the surface, nor the nodules, small at first, on ears and noses, which an experienced worker sees at first glance. Some of the older patients may be grossly maimed, without toes or fingers; they may be blind; but these are not necessarily the most infectious. The so-called 'burnt-out cases' are usually those which have never had medical treatment, in whose bodies the disease has finally worked itself out. Ronald Heald, the remarkable man in charge of the leper work at Newala and Lulindi and of all the out-patient clinics in the Masasi diocese (a work begun by Edith Shelley, a medical missionary who herself became a leper, and now carried on under the Universities Mission to Central Africa) told me that a symptom which causes great trouble is the loss of feeling in a leprous limb; patients returning to their villages, where rats abound, are told to cover their feet at night with baskets or chicken-netting, and in spite of this many of them have their toes eaten. He showed me the Lulindi clinic in operation, opening the ragged garments of his patients with the tender readiness to handle infected flesh which is one of the marks of the leprophil, indicating patches, discolorations, nodules, pronouncing the word 'leprous' with a lingering, almost poetic intonation, as though for the adept its meaning were esoteric. It was touching to see how the old men and even the women and children pulled open their clothing and bowed their heads to display the stigma of leprosy to the visitor. I had the feeling that they knew themselves out of the common and worthy of note, as though the signs they carried, even the elusive odour, faintly aromatic, corruptly sweet, were compensations in a life sufficiently odious and wretched. If that is so, and not my fancy, then Ronald Heald and his kind have done more for their lepers than bring them drugs and treatment and return them to life. They have embraced them in a fashion that weakens the ancient concept of the leper as outcast, which, however baseless in the light of modern knowledge, still keeps its witch's authority in continents supposedly far less dark than Africa.

IX

MISSIONARIES AND MAXIMS

IONIDES' distrust of missionaries, which is obstinate and impersonal, is only one aspect of an instinctive disapproval of everything called progress, which he prefers to define as interference with the natural course of life. He does not care for the changes which western civilization has brought to Africa, though he is rather more kindly disposed to Arab influence, and believes that primitive peoples are best left alone to work out their destiny through the stages to which evolution has gradually brought them. He is realistic enough to admit that this is impossible, and that one cannot put back the clock; but this does not reconcile him to the forced pace of change which he sees everywhere in Africa, and he might well say with the poet, 'I know. But I do not approve. And I am not resigned.' He cannot bring himself to agree that the tribes around him are happier or better off than in the days when their prime occupation was tribal warfare. 'These people have been largely emasculated, that's what it amounts to. Their splendid virtues have been driven out of them; it isn't their fault if we've turned them into a rather second-rate lot. Tribal wars gave them a far more interesting and invigorating time than they can hope to have again. What did they amount to after all? In the course of a good feud perhaps six people got killed, and all the rest were kept on their toes and had fresh air and exercise.' (Stanley, writing of tribal warfare in Tanganyika in the late eighteen-sixties, calls it 'a tame way of fighting, after all'. One chief, he says, 'makes a raid into another's country, and succeeds in making off with a herd of cattle, killing one or two men who have been surprised. Weeks, or perhaps months elapse before the other retaliates, and effects a capture in a similar way, and then a balance is struck in which neither is the gainer'.) It is clear that no amount of effort on Ionides' part could bring his views into line with those of the missionaries.

One morning soon after the cobra-dig at the hospital I had persuaded him to go with me into one of the Indian stores in Newala, to make some small purchase (a thing he is normally most unwilling to do, shopping being a task more fittingly performed by Makabui) and we had been surprised to find two English ladies there before us, buying groceries for the mission school at Lulindi. Introductions were somehow made, to which Ionides responded with a reserved bow and the kind of smile which shows all his lower teeth, and cannot, except by the unwary, be associated with pleasure. They were, of course, missionaries, and the encounter, which had been outwardly civil, started a train of thought to which he returned next day, when, it being Sunday, with the bell of the Catholic mission faintly tolling, we were alternately busy and idle with the snake-packing. 'I don't believe missionaries do much good, do you?' he said mildly, watching from his chair while Rashidi, in surprising Sabbath costume of red gingham skirt and a dinner-jacket, was carrying the crates, cardboard boxes, calico bags and tongs necessary for the operation. 'Of course one may be prejudiced, being on the wrong side of the fence. They make me feel that one's regarded as the Enemy. I was once described as Anti-Christ by a Roman Catholic padre, who crossed himself as he said it; a title of which I was naturally very proud.'

Ionides himself was brought up in the Greek Orthodox Church, which he considers sensible and tolerant as churches go; but at the age of ten he lost his faith, and nothing since has encouraged him to recover it. 'I was at prep-school then, you know, never questioning what I was taught in religious matters. It had simply never occurred to me to do so. We had plenty of religious teaching at school—Church of England, of course—and I implicitly believed that if one prayed for something hard enough, and one's faith were perfect, one would certainly get it. That was what we were told; the important thing was faith; and I devoutly believed it. Well, one day a friend and I, being pretty fed up and miserable at school—it was a beastly place, you know—decided, having been to the zoo together in the holidays, that what we wanted from God was to be changed into tigers in the Indian jungle. We had both been told, and implicitly believed, that if you had faith, even as a grain of mustard seed, you could move mountains. We didn't want anything like that, but we *did* want to escape from school by being changed into tigers. So on a Saturday—I even remember the day, it was such a terrific decision—we made this pact, and I got down on my knees at my bedside and absolutely prayed, with complete faith, that instead of being routed by that blasted bell and being plunged into a filthy cold bath in mid-winter, I should wake up in a nice Indian jungle as a tiger. Well, I duly went to sleep. To my horror I was wakened by the same bell, had the same cold bath; and although, looking in the glass in the early light, I thought for a moment that the wrinkling of my forehead was the beginning of stripes, I could see that it hadn't worked. At the earliest opportunity I got hold of this friend of mine and complained to him. He said, "That's all right, don't worry; I've been thinking it over, and I've come to the conclusion that to ask God to work on a Sunday is unreasonable. Let it go for another day, and then we'll try again." I saw the force of this, so we dragged through the day somehow, and in the evening I got down on my knees and prayed like hell to wake up as an Indian tiger. When that bell rang again, that finished me for religion.'

This childish story is naïve enough, perhaps, but the experience left its mark, and laid the foundation of a fierce intolerance of the fairy-tale element in conventional religion from which he has never since deviated. 'I hate humbug,' he says, and since many of the spiritual promises made by missionaries to Africans seem to him to come under this heading, and to be quite as delusive as the ancestor-worship and magic of their own religions, he regards all proselytizing with suspicion as part of the white man's campaign to undermine, emasculate, and control the African. His experience of army padres in the Second World War did nothing to weaken this opinion; if anything it reinforced it, for their efforts to impose an alien and impossible sexual morality on the African askaris struck him as 'a deliberate and contemptible shutting of the eyes to reality'. Ionides had temporarily left the Game Department for the army in 1941, and being considered too old for service overseas had been sent to Abyssinia, where African troops were stationed in great numbers, although the fighting in that area was over. 'The trouble was, these men at home had been used to having their women good and regular, and now they had none. During the fighting this hadn't worried them much, but now they had nothing to do, and were kept in a barbed-wire compound like a lot of goats. There'd been some ugly incidents, and I saw there'd be real trouble if nothing was done. I therefore persuaded the C.O. to let all the men who were not on guard go out at night, provided they got a chit from the M.O. afterwards, certifying that they'd had prophylactic treatment. The tension relaxed immediately under this new arrangement, but the padre blew up in righteous indignation and wanted it stopped. According to him it was an insult to his Christians to order them to submit to preventive treatment, when naturally they wouldn't think of breaking the commandments. I must say it made me very happy to send for the V.D. dossier and show the padre his Christians topping the list.'

The conversation was interrupted at this point by Rashidi announcing that everything was ready, and Ionides rose to pack the week's catch. We had an unusually large number of puff-adders this week, some of them young males which for several evenings had kept up a sort of slow-motion wrestling-match, apparently caused by the presence of a nearby female. He had several times, he said, watched these mating contests carried on in captivity; they usually kept it up until they were tired, or until one of the snakes, scoring some mysterious point over his opponent, established superiority. He had never seen puff-adders bite one another, though he had known boomslangs do it, sinking their poison-fangs deeply into the flesh, so that the wounds bled; the curious thing was that they always survived, showing no serious effects from these vicious bites. (Cautious as always, Ionides does not deduce from this that all venomous snakes are immune from each other's poison; he suspects only that snakes of the same species, secreting the same venom, may possibly be so.) The puff-adders this morning, with one exception, made no fuss. Though often extremely angry at the moment of capture they are surprisingly tolerant about being put into bags, and seem almost to welcome the change from the comfortless box. The system of transferring them, though it requires some skill, is simple. A tall cardboard carton is placed on the floor and the open calico bag suspended inside it, clipped to the sides of the carton with two pairs of tongs. Each box is then opened in turn and the snake prised up with a stick with a club-shaped end, and lifted across, like a worm on a gardening-fork, dangling above the mouth of the open bag. Usually the snakes pour hopefully forward at once, tongue flickering, eyes steady and bright, while Rashidi or Pétu supports the hinder part on another stick. Once the head is manœuvred inside the bag they slide into it readily enough, dropping with a soft plop when the sticks are withdrawn; the tape is swiftly drawn up and knotted before they have time to turn round, the bag being lifted up with the metal tongs and the heavy load transferred to the travelling box. Big snakes are packed singly, smaller ones in pairs; they seem to have no objection to travelling companions and do each other no damage. The gaboon vipers are the heaviest, and seemed often abstracted during the operation, hanging placid and motionless in mid-air while they ran their black and rose-pink tongues back and forth and gazed ahead in a vacant trance-like stare. Sometimes they would go anywhere but into the bag, swinging the head aside at the crucial moment, diving heavily between the bag and the box, or even, in a burst of energy, pouring clean off the sticks to fall with a smack on the floor and wind away under the table; but in the end the head was steered in the right direction, the snake surged smoothly downwards into cover, and with the help of a hand the body was toppled after. Only one, a puff-adder, attempted to retaliate, striking sideways at Ionides in mid-air as he juggled it cautiously forward into the bag; but his evasive movement was fully as quick as the snake's and there was only a momentary flash of jaws, of fangs hinged suddenly forward like the teeth of a rake, before he had caught it by the tail and given it a shake. Before it could right itself it was already in the bag, vanished from sight like a body dropped down a well, and Rashidi was calmly drawing and knotting the tapes.

It is easy to see, when one watches this apparently effortless handling, why it is that many Africans (though not Rashidi and Pétu, who are both fairly adept) believe that Ionides has some special magical control over venomous snakes, which may even be turned on themselves if they are not careful. He does nothing to encourage this belief; he also takes no trouble to deny it; there are occasions when a reputation is useful. 'It is sometimes convenient,' he said, when the dragging about of wooden boxes on the cement floor had made conversation in the house impossible, and we had moved to the veranda to warm ourselves in the hot sun, 'to have people believe that it may be, shall we say *inadvisable* to displease one. I don't lay any stress on it, but on the other hand I don't wear myself out in an effort to convince them that it isn't true. They'll believe it, whether or not. It's easier than working out the simple relationship of cause and effect, and more exciting. Magic is perfectly natural to these people'.

We had taken the little sand-snake into the sun with us, and she was peacefully uncoiling herself across his knees. The cook's chickens, a hen with a scrawny and enterprising family, were picking about at our feet, and it seemed to me that the snake was not unobservant.

'When they see me catch a snake—often a harmless one, which they ought to know perfectly well—and I let it travel over my hands, they say at once, "But why doesn't it bite you? It must be because of your magic!" They also think that the reason the gaboon vipers remain sleepy and sluggish when I catch them is *not* because they're very placid snakes, but because I employ some sorcery to keep them asleep. When I touch them with the tongs to judge the reaction, *they* think that touch with the tongs is a sort of soporific. They even believed in the old days, when I used to track lion into thickets and find them asleep, that the only reason they remained so was because I'd put a spell on them. It didn't occur to them that the animals were sleeping like pigs because they were gorged, and didn't hear me because I was jolly careful. They used to try and buy my magic—still do as a matter of fact.'

'Where do they think you keep it?'

'Some people think it's in that box of books, the one beside our chairs, which I always pack myself. Then in the days when I used to wear a very old battered hat, a lot of people thought the magic was in that. The hat became a sort of gimmick, you know, a trade-mark. I've still got it somewhere, and they occasionally ask to see it. Then one of my forked sticks at one time, I believe, was suspect as an implement of magic. It doesn't matter what it is; they'll pick on anything.'

'Do they think your magic has power over human beings?'

'So far as I can make out, they think I have some sort of *subconscious* sorcerer's power. The way it has been put to me is that my "tongue is bad". What they mean by that is . . . well, one's lived in this country for a long time, and in the nature of things a certain number of people with whom one gets angry die almost immediately afterwards.'

'Oh, *do* they?'

'Yes, I've had a bit of luck on several occasions. Twice, when I happened to have been *really* angry with certain people, each time the man was shot with a poisoned arrow very soon afterwards, and it was thought to be a direct result of displeasing Father. It isn't when I fly into a rage and swear at them, but when I'm quite quiet and *really* angry, that this is suspected. Accidents *have* happened to people shortly after I've been annoyed with them, and it's somehow attributed to this subconscious bewitching. I don't think, you know, they really imagine I *deliberately* cast spells or pray people to death, but simply that as a result of my displeasure funny things happen.'

The snake by this time was growing too lively with the sun or the presence of the chickens, and he shifted her gently to his shoulders, where she explored the hollow of an ear with her tendril tongue.

'Would you be afraid to curse somebody in public, just in case something . . . what you call *funny* happened?'

'Not in the least. I do it frequently.'

'You haven't any belief, then, in your own magic?'

'None whatever. I wish I *had* mysterious powers, because then a lot of unmentionable people would be dead. Or shall I mention them, perhaps?'

'No, better not.'

The boxes were now brought out to the veranda one by one, each sewn into a tight cover of stout sacking. Each was identified and inspected, and the correct labels, which Ionides had prepared, firmly sewn to the sacking in his presence. I was puzzled to see that the boxes, irrespective of what they contained, were plainly marked 'Live Snakes: value 2/-.' 'Ah, that,' he said, 'is because a lot of them are going to America, and American air lines charge according to the value, and in case of death or damage never pay. It's almost unknown to lose a snake going to Switzerland, but the Americans stink. They're rough and careless handlers; they just don't care. A consignment of mine was once kept hanging about between New York and Miami for over three weeks and nearly all the snakes died. Proper swine.'

My mind was still on his reputation for magic, for I could well see, having inwardly cringed on several occasions when a blast of fury had withered Makanga after some trivial mistake, when he had failed to bring the mustard with the sausage, or when my onions, which I liked chopped, had for some inscrutable reason been presented whole, in their skins, that a simple mind would find it hard to believe that no evil curse was implicit in such an outburst. Ionides, however, to my surprise, claimed that I had never seen him really angry, which left me quite fearfully wondering. I had already noticed that such manifestations as took place in my presence were soon over, and as far as I was concerned, living at close quarters with him now for several weeks, I had rarely encountered a gentler or more equable temperament. It was a puzzle, for the irascibility was both real and violent, and he seemed to make no effort to control it.

'That is deliberate,' he said, when I tentatively questioned him. 'A hot temper has always been my curse. I have discovered, by experience, that I am incapable of properly controlling it. I am, however, able to repress it. *If* I repress it, it goes bad on me, and then it really does get unpleasant, evil and sulky and nasty. (Oh, you've never really heard me go off; I hope you won't.) I have found that, *for me*, the only expedient is to give way to this weakness and blow it out quite harmlessly. It *is* a weakness. One makes a fool of oneself periodically by doing so; it must detract from one's authority and the respect that people feel for one; but it's the better of two alternatives.'

'Well, I don't know that it does detract from your authority, at least in Africa. I have the impression, with your own people, that when you point out deficiencies in a particularly menacing tone of voice they jump to it in a way that I suspect they mightn't do with a milder man.'

'It may be so. I don't know. There may be a great resentment concealed, but they never show it. When I was ill some time ago Makanga showed a rather touching concern; looked after me like a baby.'

'But if you could change one thing in your nature, would it be that? Would you prefer not to have this hot temper, if you could choose?'

There was a pause, while the last of the finished boxes was brought out for inspection and carried off in the direction of the lorry.

'I'm not . . . sure. I would choose, rather, to have proper control of my temper. To be able to think straight whatever the situation, however angry I happened to feel inside. But I also think that if I had too sweet a temper I should lose some virtue. I doubt whether I could hunt so fiercely and persistingly the animals I wanted, or pursue my aims quite so single-mindedly.'

'In fact you might become less like Genghis Khan, or Timor, or Alexander the Great?' He bowed his head in the usual grave movement of assent, the corners of his mouth curved in the beginnings of a smile.

'There might be fewer pyramids of skulls. Possibly.'

There have been times in the past, however, when the violence of his nature has led him into severities that he now regrets. Incidents are still remembered in Tanganyika which he would prefer to have forgotten; the flogging of a whole village on one shocking occasion, and on another the knocking down of a village head-man, who lost five of his teeth.

'Looking back, I think now that I rather overdid it. More *kiboko* than was really necessary, you know.' (Kiboko, being Swahili for hippopotamus, refers also to a lash made from the animal's hide, a traditional African instrument of discipline.) 'But they were often very difficult and obstructive to the Game Department. In fact, one had to be tough.'

The famous flogging had been the climax of one of those maddening complexes of frustration when, as usual, the Game Ranger had been called in to deal with trouble from man-eating lions or marauding elephants, and the village concerned, while clamouring for aid, had refused to carry gear or to build a hut to accommodate their local game-scout. The refusal to carry was a favourite gambit, porterage having always been an unpopular form of labour; Stanley's and Burton's narratives are full of crises over porters, of food-bales lost or stolen, of packs thrown down as absconders sprinted for the bush. This village had also, in defiance of the most stringent prohibitions, persisted in ambushing water-holes and slaughtering large numbers of buffalo with poisoned arrows, and there had come a point where Ionides' rage had exploded and he had decided that only a demonstration of frightfulness would get results. Accordingly the adult males of the village, all sixty of them, had been ordered a flogging which was administered by the game-scouts. The men had received it philosophically and the game-scouts enjoyed themselves. 'There was no more trouble after that. It was only necessary, when obstruction seemed likely, to hang *kiboko* over the door of my hut.'

The assault on the head-man might have led to serious official trouble for Ionides, but the man himself made only one abortive complaint, and relations were apparently even improved by the incident. Again it was a case of exasperating obstruction. Ionides had been called in by the District Commissioner to hunt out some man-eating lions which were terrorizing a village in the neighbourhood of Lindi. The village was reached after four hours' walk through the bush, and the spoor of a big lion was identified. Tracking went on for some days without result, for the spoor, which at first had been clear and fresh, disappeared in a mysterious manner overnight. The puzzle was explained when one of the game-scouts, creeping through a thicket, came upon the head-man of the village carefully hoeing a patch of ground which had been covered with tracks, with the object of misleading Ionides and sending him off to search in another area. This was the time of the year when the crops are in and there is no shortage; the man simply preferred to drive the lions away for the time being, or even to put up with them, rather than have the nuisance of the Game Ranger and his men demanding help and millet from the neighbourhood. Ionides' immediate reaction had been to order a flogging, but he knew that the man had a hernia, and contented himself with a right hook to the jaw, knocking out five teeth and embedding one of them painfully in his knuckle. After that, it seems, there was co-operation, and the villagers set about producing food, carrying baggage and generally assisting in the lion-hunt. The head-man did, some time afterwards, report the matter to the local African policeman, who told him to keep his mouth shut and consider himself lucky. (The man-eaters, after all, had been eventually shot.) Ionides meanwhile, having extracted the tooth from his hand, which was now septic, had the annoyance of having to go into the Lindi hospital, where it was lanced and stitched. The District Commissioner heard the story by chance, and wrote 'a most offensive letter, full of blood and fire and threats', but by this time the matter had been forgotten, or at least had turned into one of those legends of which the head-man was rather proud. He had become, strange to say, one of the dreaded Game Ranger's keenest partisans.

This natural acceptance of sudden and short-lived reprisals, as opposed to more protracted and civilized methods of justice, is an aspect of African character which encourages Ionides not to reproach himself too seriously over past incidents. Nowadays it is a different matter (though one hears of *kiboko* being reintroduced by more than one newly appointed African Commissioner) but in the past it was accepted as being often the only way of getting things done. 'As recently as 1955, when two of my game-scouts had committed serious offences, instead of disciplining them by the old method I recommended their dismissal from the service and this was done. An indignation meeting was immediately held, and Makabui, who always acts as go-between in such matters, came to me and said, "Why are you now so harsh to your own people? In the old days you would have given Game Department punishment, and nothing more would have been thought of it." I said to him, "In the old days you looked on me as your father. This is so no longer. I can show you a whole file of complaints from official quarters on this subject. The culprits may not like it. Neither do I. But it is easier for me to dismiss a man and keep the law." The District Commissioners, he pointed out, had never had this sort of obstructive behaviour to contend with because they travelled with armed askaris and were His Majesty's representatives. The Game Ranger and his scouts were easy to defy, and to prove that defiance did not pay was often most effectively done by primitive methods.

Some of Ionides' simplicities, however, are incomprehensible to Africans; even Makabui, who would claim to be unprejudiced and sophisticated, was deeply shocked by his instructions for his own burial. It is his firm wish that when he dies, which he hopes and believes will be in Tanganyika, there shall be no funeral service of any sort and that his body shall be left in the bush to be eaten by jackals. 'Death is so utterly unimportant; the body, when it is finished with, so useless. I strongly object to being a nuisance after I'm dead. I've been a carnivore all my life, and I'd much rather benefit a few local vultures and jackals than go against nature and have all the nonsense of a conventional burial. I tried,' he said wistfully, raising thick eyebrows and looking mildly aggrieved, 'to have it put in my will when I was in London a few years ago, but the solicitor refused. Why should he refuse to meet such a simple request? I asked the D.C. here, too, and my own servants; but they wouldn't hear of it. They were all shocked to the core. I hate humbug.'

Whatever the solicitor may have thought I doubt whether the servants' refusal could fairly be called humbug, for Africans have strong beliefs concerning death and burial, and to be put out for the jackals and kites would seem to them a shameful end and fit only for a malefactor. In Tanganyika, whatever they may do elsewhere, they bury their dead, and the spirit of a powerful and respected man, as Ionides is, is considered to keep its power for a long while, and like those of the Pharaohs of Egypt to inhabit the grave. The graves of men, though not of women, are marked with a planted tree, often in the middle of a village where offerings can be left, advice asked, aid invoked. One can imagine Ionides' spirit being wooed if a plague of cobras should ever discomfit Newala, and no doubt to abandon him to the jackals would be more than enough to invite the most punitive visitations. They would rather inter him decently, with his tongs and his snake-sticks, in the worn-out jersey and plimsolls that they remember. Chiefs are buried with their weapons, rich men with rolls of cloth; Ionides' magic hat, perhaps, would serve. Only lepers, I was told, are buried naked.

Ionides has no religious beliefs, but the consistency of his behaviour suggests that there is an immediate reference to some private code, and if one questions him about ethics he conscientiously hesitates.

'I don't deliberately subscribe to any code, if that's what you mean. Such code as I have—and it's a word I don't like using because I'm a great believer in judging everything on its merits—such things as you could *almost* call rules are based simply on intelligence; intelligence implemented by habit of mind. That's to say, I think they were originally based on intelligence, and then one got in the habit of doing a certain thing, and felt uncomfortable if one didn't do it.'

'Without regard, do you mean, to the comfort and feelings of other people?'

'No, the intelligence is wholly concerned with the comfort and feelings of other people, which are bound to react on oneself. That is the point of the thing. In general, so far as I have been able to make out, in the vast majority of cases anti-social behaviour is inexpedient and foolish. It is simply more stupid and short-sighted than anything else. Now, to give you an example of something that I think very important—a name for integrity is an extremely valuable possession. I've had that proved to me many and many a time. To lose it for the sake of some momentary advantage—to break your word, in short—I cannot think at all, I never *have* been able to think of circumstances in which that would pay. I therefore long ago reached the stage where if I broke my word, even quite trivially, to anyone, I should feel horribly uncomfortable. But behind it all, I think, would be the conviction that I'd been a bloody fool, rather than that I'd done anything wrong. That's as far as I can say, consciously. So far as I'm concerned there are no absolutes. Surely we all live, if you get down to the basis of behaviour, on the principle of "You scratch my back, I'll scratch yours"? That may not be a pretty way of putting it; your friends at the mission would possibly not approve of it; but you'll find that principle, in some form or other, implicit in most religions. Now in the bush it is always expedient to be helpful to other people, and they are (or should be) reciprocally helpful to you. This happens in wars, and in hard countries, the frozen north for example, in which, to be able to survive, you *must* help one another. Do unto others, and so on. Today, me; tomorrow, possibly, you.'

'Would you then call yourself an atheist?'

'Oh no. Emphatically not. My observations of nature

have shown—at least they have convinced *me*—that there must be some guiding force which I personally prefer to call Nature but which can equally well be called God, but *some* guiding force which runs this universe. One has only to observe after the dry season, when there's nothing but scorched, dry, bare earth, how the rain falls, the grass grows, birds and animals mate and breed, and you see all the wonderful healing processes of nature. To describe oneself as an atheist is to suggest that all this comes about purely by blind chance. And that seems to me a quite untenable position.

'Although,' he went on, careful as always to close a gap which might lead to an ambiguous conclusion, 'although I believe in this force which directs everything, I've never considered it to have the slightest connection with moral behaviour, or necessarily to be interested in the human animal more than in any others; and I cannot convince myself that one can communicate with this force in any way, let alone influence it.'

'You would never, I take it, pray?'

'Oh *yes*, I've prayed on many an occasion; reverted to pure atavism. I remember once . . .' (and here the example, so gravely offered, was of just that deflating description that the question deserved) '. . . when I was following up on the red-hot spoor of a bongo, which was an animal I had been hunting for four months, I suddenly felt the wind on the back of my neck, and I found myself praying to some God in a frenzy of fear, praying for the wind to change. But it had no genuine faith or anything else behind it; only terror.'

'And did the wind change, do you remember, as it did for Joan of Arc?'

'It did not. The blasted bongo got away.'

Though it would be futile to try and deduce any code of behaviour from his beliefs and opinions, one might, with some patience, extract a set of maxims from Ionides, for he applies to life the scientific method proper to nature study, and proposes nothing that he has not been convinced of by experience. He does not discourage such an inquiry, though he may doubt its usefulness; it is the first of his axioms never to discourage anybody—'Life will do that soon enough'. It is easy at first, listening to the ready flow of his talk, to conclude him pessimistic or even cynical, but he is simply realistic, refusing to suppose anything about human nature which, from his observations, is at odds with the evidence. 'For years I've taken nature notes on the human animal, as on other species that have come my way, and a conclusion I have come to is that one must never expect too much of human beings. Always expect people to act as self-interest dictates, and you won't be unduly embittered when you're let down. It's a lack of knowledge of the human animal which makes one surprised and angry. You should *expect* to be let down in the normal way; you have jam on it when you're not. It makes me sick to hear Europeans complain, as they often do, of being let down by Africans; one frequently hears of the base ingratitude of these people. What have they got to be grateful for, I should like to know? An African may be your paid servant, but his first loyalties are to his wife and family; it's foolish to expect unreasonably faithful service, as it is to look for immaculate faithfulness from one's friends. Where there's some falling off we should admit, if we were quite honest, that the fault is our own, in setting too high a standard for other people. People don't, you notice, invariably set them for themselves.'

This attitude makes him exceptionally tolerant, in spite of his outbursts of irritability, which are short-lived. He accepts people, as he accepts animals, for what they are, and scorns pretence as much as he despises excuses. He takes full responsibility for his actions, for failure as well as success, and is impatient of any talk of bad luck, which he does not believe in. 'If I were to give any advice to the young, one of the first things I would say would be, "Never complain of bad luck; at least not consistently." In my experience most of our good or bad luck, so called, our successes or failures, are due wholly to ourselves. It is very unprofitable to moan; to say, Oh, it isn't fair; Oh, the world is against me; Oh, if only the wind hadn't changed, and so on. In hunting, which you can take as a sort of parable of life, the consistently successful hunter is the good hunter, the consistently unsuccessful hunter the bad one. Luck plays only a very moderate part. One is always tempted to make this excuse for failure, but that is no way to learn. In that elephant mauling I told you about there was no bad luck involved, it was just bad hunting. I should have observed things that I didn't observe; I was careless and wholly to blame. But I learned from the incident, and *insh'Allah*—God willing—I shall go on learning. "The fault, dear Brutus, is not in our stars, But in ourselves. . . ." I so often think of that.'

'And if you were to offer a second piece of advice to the young—or to anyone else for that matter—what would it be?'

'I am not in the habit of offering advice, but since you ask I think it would be, "Never allow yourself to be deterred, by apparently great difficulties, from achieving something you really wish to achieve." It is important to remember that we are creatures of habit, and persistence can be cultivated. For instance, I remember, when I first went alone into the Congo to start elephant-poaching'—he was quite free, of course, from any notion that advice to the young must necessarily be of an elevating character—'I had no idea at all how to set about it; it all seemed extremely difficult and the temptation to funk it was immense. But I soon found that as soon as I actually did it, though I might or might not make a hash of a particular enterprise, the difficulties did largely melt away, and that helped me very greatly with the next problem. The next time you go for this thing, this achievement, you find that the difficulties are not quite so great as they seemed, until in the latter end you take them in your stride. Whereas I have an idea that if you allow yourself to be intimidated once, or anyway twice, you end up by doing nothing, and then very likely moan about it afterwards and say you never had a chance.'

'I believe you admire moral courage.'

'Why, of course. Every sort of courage is invaluable. Like that friend of yours that you were telling me about. Some rather well-known man, I believe, I don't remember his name? Who sat in the street to do with the atomic bomb. Bert Something, I think you said his name was? He seemed to me to have the right ideas for survival.'

'Could you mean Bertrand Russell?'

'That might have been the name. It wasn't familiar to me, but then I never read the newspapers. But it struck me, from what you said, that he had moral courage. The human animal *must* have that, if it wants to go on living. It's a natural weapon, after all, like venom to the cobra. Indispensable.'

X

A DEARTH OF PYTHONS

THERE was still no news of a python. The sand-snake being now as tame as one could reasonably wish, we wanted to try our hand on something bigger, and the unaccountable absence of pythons began to fret us. Normally Ionides does not bother with them, but he has caught many in the past and tamed a few with success, and to have one in the house for my last few weeks, setting it free when I finally left for England, was an undertaking we had set our hearts on. The trouble was that pythons had not for a long time been quoted on the snake-tariff, and no one was in the habit of reporting them. Snake-catching as a workable system takes a long time to establish, and Ionides was pessimistic. If we had several months to spare we should be sure to get one; after a sufficient lapse of time, when the idea had penetrated, pythons of every size would be heard of all over the area, particularly near the river; it was wanting one in a hurry that was unfortunate.

I proposed that we should go down to the Ruvuma ourselves, for I was tantalized by that pewter streak in the distance, only twelve miles away, with hills beyond which I knew were Mozambique. Three years before, I had been in that country, hunting for treasure, and though I would not have cared to return by any official route (since my presence there had been furtive and my entry unobserved) I longed at least to go down to our side of the river, perhaps even to cross by canoe and set foot if only for a moment on foreign sand. Relations between Tanganyika and Mozambique were at the moment politically disagreeable, as they probably still are, and there was no official coming and going between the two territories, though natives on both sides continued to cross by canoe whenever it suited them. I did not see why, since a single canoe was unlikely to attract notice, we should not make at least a brief and picnic-spirited expedition.

But Ionides was adamant. It was not so much, I found, that he was against the idea of crossing without permission as that the whole notion of going down to the river at all was impracticable after the long rains, and would in any case be futile. If no python had been reported, we would find none. Even if the swamps near the river were crawling with them we would get no news, twelve miles of bush without passable roads being too great a distance for a news-bearer to cover. We would do better to stay where we were, broadcast the news that a python was wanted, and wait. He had already sent out word, more than once, that he would pay several pounds for news of a good python, and nothing had happened. Why did I think that our going to the river ourselves, and getting the Land Rover stuck in a morass, would make any difference?

I brooded over this for some days, while Ionides, who had no objection to my going with a suitable companion if I could find one, provided he were not himself forced into this fool's errand, sent out messages in various directions to inquire into the state of the roads. I had once been to the very edge of the escarpment at Makote, ten miles away, with the handsome Danish engineer from the waterworks, and we had climbed a crag and seen the river only a few miles off, dwindling daily between its banks with the advance of the dry season. It seemed extraordinary that one could not just drive from the springs at the bottom of the cliff straight through the bush to the river, but no one could tell us whether the roads were open. Neither Karl

Nielsen, the engineer, nor John Knight, the agricultural officer, had had occasion to go that way since before the rains, and they were no more willing than anyone else to risk their vehicles. As for the local Africans, they never seemed to go more than a mile or two from their own village, and their answer was always the same: they had not been down to the river for months, and knew nothing. I began to see the force of Ionides' arguments: everything in Africa takes an interminable time, and if I thought people likely to know something about the second biggest river in East Africa simply because they lived within twelve miles of it, I had better think again. In the end it was John Ambrose, the new African District Commissioner at Newala, who found out that one of the roads was said to be open, and obligingly offered to take me in his truck. I chose a Sunday, in order not to miss a morning's snake-catching, and left Ionides after breakfast, staring as usual into space with his feet on the writing-table.

Somewhere below the escarpment we picked up the local *liwali* to act as guide, and this engaging character, a charming and vivacious old man in an embroidered skull-cap, enlivened the journey with a flow of observation and anecdote which would have done credit to Ionides himself, but of which I understood nothing. ('He is a man prone to many words,' said John Ambrose in my ear, while the old man slapped his thigh and laughed, as though at a delicious compliment.) Whenever the Land Rover stopped, for stones to be laid in the mud or for a gully to be negotiated, he sprang down like a grasshopper and eagerly ran to take charge of the operation, addressing each little crowd that gathered with the air of a man who welcomes even the least promising occasion for oratory. He had his effect, too, for by the time we reached the fertile levels of the Ruvuma, where the cashew trees were loaded with flower and fruit and there were rice-fields already green with growth and pools full of water-lilies, we had a fair proportion of the population with us, chattering blithely and trotting ahead to point out the hazards, since the mud and crevasses of the road obliged us to move slowly.

It was a green and enchanted country, steamy and lush, waving with banana-palms and dotted with groups of thatched huts where women sat in the shade in timeless idleness, only languidly raising a hand as we passed to beckon their naked children. Life is easier down here than on the plateau, but sickness is rife and poverty extreme; even the flies that crawled on our faces were easily caught, seeming to share the universal lethargy. There were a few big trees still left from the primary forest, and we passed through their heavy shade with a sense of relief, for the heat was oppressive; but each one, I noticed, was blackened and scarred with fire, and many had a pyre of brushwood piled round them ready for a burning. 'It is prohibited to cut the trees without permission,' John Ambrose told me; 'there are so few left. But burning is not cutting, as you see, and they destroy them in this manner. Then they can plead that the tree caught fire by accident, while clearing the shamba.'

At last we reached the edge of the sand and set out on foot to traverse the dazzling dunes which hid the river. The fine hot sand poured into my sandals and made heavy walking, but when I took them off I found it far too hot for my naked foot. Only when we reached the river itself, powerfully rushing between steep banks which looked as though a tide had just receded, was I able to walk in comfort, splashing through warm pools and shallow quicksands and occasionally dipping my feet in the cooler river. I could not judge how wide the river might be; empty and silent and impressive, blossoming all over with those curious rippling disturbances of the surface which one sees only on deep and rapid water, it stretched for perhaps a mile to the opposite shore, where the same vacant dazzling dunes were repeated, lying at the foot of steeply rising woods. It was from the mouth of this same river, as I now remembered, that Livingstone had set out on his last journey, cutting his laborious way through that very jungle, wandering for seven years 'like an uneasy spirit', obsessed with his search for the fountains of the Nile.

At first the shore had seemed deserted, but now that we had crossed the last swell of sand we could see a shelter of palm-leaves near the river, and the black figures of fishermen, naked, shining and wet, wading in the shallows to pay out their fragile nets. There was a long canoe lying under the shore, a heavy black tree-trunk hollowed by tools and fire, secured by a pole and a thong against the straining current. This was one of the places where lepers and others crossed from Mozambique, and a modest business in ferrying was carried on. It was also a spot, Ionides had told me, where elephants crossed from the forest to raid the crops, swimming in herds when the flood was fast and deep, walking submerged on the bottom when the river was low, the tips of their trunks breaking the surface like periscopes. There were some sandy shoals here, which in the dry season put on growth and became islands, creating lagoons and shallow creeks where the Ruvuma method of fishing could be carried on safely. This is done by wading and swimming, paying out the nets in a wide circle and driving the fish into them by splashing and beating the surface, heading off the shoals by swimming under water. The chief danger is from crocodiles, for the best fishing is done at night, by crocodiles as well as men, and every now and again there are ugly accidents. But even so it is not considered wise to shoot out the crocodiles, since they keep down the otters and devour the biggest fish which prey on the others, performing a useful function which delights Ionides. Getting rid of the crocodiles, he likes to point out, actually deteriorates the fishing, just as rats will multiply round a village where snakes are destroyed. Facts of this description, which support his empirical view of the balance of nature, give him extreme satisfaction.

Fishing on this particular day was rather half-hearted and the catch small, for the river was still too high and strong for swimming and the nets were in poor condition. When John Ambrose and the *liwali* were caught sight of the fishermen came in from the shallows and crowded round us, hoping that we brought them some nylon nets which they were badly in need of. Finding that we did not, they scraped out their reed fish-traps, long bottle-shaped baskets carried on their shoulders, and showed us the few little flapping fish that they had got for their trouble. Asked about pythons they replied as usual that there were plenty in the area—oh, big ones, yes, and so numerous that one might suppose it difficult to walk a yard without treading on them; but when John Ambrose questioned them closely it also transpired, as usual, that no one had seen one lately. There was a hippo and her calf, they said hopefully, in the little lake with blue water-lilies that we had passed half a mile back, but as to pythons they could not exactly say. Tomorrow, perhaps, or next week, they would be sure to find one; no doubt we would come again. It was clear that Ionides' pessimism was well founded, and that however much I might enjoy my glimpse of the Ruvuma the day's outing would have no other result. There was nothing more to be done, except perhaps to cross to the other side, which I yearned to do; the dug-out canoe looked strong, and Mozambique not more than a mile away. But here other difficulties presented themselves; John Ambrose could not swim, and in his clean white shirt and shorts and horn-rimmed spectacles was unwilling to risk himself on the water, while the *liwali*, who was perfectly game for a small outing, pointed out that it would never do for him to set foot on Portuguese territory. He might be seen, and this would constitute an incident. Askaris, he said, sometimes patrolled the river in motor-launches, and though the opposite shore looked empty enough we might be sure that we were watched. So in the end he and I lowered ourselves gingerly into the wet bottom of the canoe and were edged skilfully upstream for perhaps a quarter of a mile, the boatman propelling the heavy carcase with vigorous sweeps of his long pole until finally, having reached the middle of the river, where the force of the current drove a glassy bank of water against our bow, he swung the canoe round, manœuvring his long pole in an exquisite balance, and brought us plunging and bouncing back to shore. The crowd on the bank by this time was very conspicuous, a straggling knot of black on the white sand, and I could see that by anyone abroad on the opposite hills we should be easily observed. The visit to the Ruvuma had been no more, after all, than a Sunday outing. I had neither crossed the river nor heard the faintest whisper of news of a python.

*

As the time drew near for my leaving Newala our thoughts turned to the possibility of trying for a python in a quite different area. That at least was the excuse on which we leaned, but the truth was that we were both secretly dismayed by the thought that our private interlude was coming to an end. I had promised myself, when I had touched the island for a moment on the outward journey, that I would return to Mafia, where I had seen the coral reefs and longed to explore them, and it now occurred to us that we might go together. The plan was attractive to me for several reasons, for not only was I anxious to postpone the moment of leaving Ionides, whom I might never see again, but I also continued to worry about his health, and thought that a brief spell in a warmer climate might be good for him. His cough was atrocious, though the sleeping-pills I had begged from the kind sisters at the mission, and their special cough-mixture, had improved his nights. He seemed even thinner than when I first arrived, if that were possible, and tired more easily; I had several times tried to persuade him to return with me as far as Dar-es-Salaam to see a doctor. This he refused to do, protesting that he had little use for doctors, that the cough was due to smoking, and that he was quite indifferent as to what went on in his lungs. 'I frankly don't care. The only thing I'm afraid of is living too long.' But a spell on Mafia tempted him, the more so as he had always heard that the island was noted for pythons.

We began to explore the ground by sending complicated messages over the police radio to a famous deep-sea fisherman called H. B. Swann, of whom we had both heard, and whom we knew to be in charge of a small and comfortable fishing-club on the island. If anyone were likely to help us, he was the man. The messages took a long time to compose, being necessarily complex, since pythons are nothing to do with deep-sea fishing and we could not afford to fly with a lot of equipment. We would have no vehicle, no snake-boxes, no camping gear, and wanted to make sure that some of these things could be lent to us on the island. There was, besides, the question of the news-network, which would have to be improvised at short notice and over which Ionides was naturally dubious. But we were both of us secretly determined to go, whatever the outcome, and when a message eventually came from Swann saying that pythons were certainly there though he could guarantee nothing, and that transport and camping equipment could be arranged, we fell at once into a fever of packing. That is, Ionides packed his books and some special snake-sticks, while Makabui and the rest ran about for several days on breathless errands, and an unspeakable leather hold-all, which all this time had lain in a corner of my bedroom and which I had taken for a pile of skins, was dragged out and dusted and partly filled with Ionides' gear and clothing. It was arranged that we should spend a night at Nachingwea with Norman Horsley, who had passed through Newala some days before with his game-scouts. We would go this far with the Land Rover and the lorry and all Ionides' servants and their families, leaving only the caretaker, and fly on alone to Mafia the following morning, leaving them behind. It was time, Ionides said, to pull up one's roots; he would send the lot of them north, and when I left Africa for good he would go on safari. Once we had our python, the thing that he felt the need of was an Egyptian cobra; he had had enough of Newala in the cold weather and would go off for several months into Kenya and Uganda.

The long dusty journey to Nachingwea was unmemorable, save that we were packed in more tightly than usual, with solemn-eyed children being sick on the luggage; but it was pleasant to drop through the hills into warmer air. Ionides' cough was quieter, and not even the derelict appearance of Nachingwea (once planned on a grandiose scale with streets and avenues, which with the failure of the ground-nut scheme have come to nothing) could diminish our enjoyment. At Norman Horsley's house, however, we found ourselves alone. He had been called out suddenly on lion-control, and had gone off to a village on the Ruvuma which was being terrorized by a man-eater. Everything had been left ready; the bungalow, which was a government one, met my acclimatized eye as quite splendidly comfortable. There was modern plumbing, which had once worked; on the porch some ancient garden chairs with cushions; and an almost naked frangipani tree dropping its last leaves and scented waxen flowers over the veranda. It seemed at once like home; the snake-sticks and the tongs were carefully laid out and Makanga could be heard banging about in the kitchen. Only one detail gave Ionides pause. When the meal was ready we ate from china plates, and this, it seems, was effeminate for a bachelor. What did Norman want with china plates? What was the matter with enamel? Enamel could be packed at a moment's notice and did not get broken. He pushed his meat about scornfully with a fork, relenting only when he reflected, as he did presently, that the plates, like the rest of the furniture, went with the house. Norman's character was re-established. The stuff had been foisted on him by the government.

All the same, the address of a doctor in Dar-es-Salaam, which Norman had added at the end of his explanatory note, was passed over in silence. Ionides' medical history has not been uneventful, but doctors have had no part in it until the thrombosis in the right leg took him by surprise some years ago. He has had malaria more times than he can count, amoebic dysentery, relapsing fever from the bite of a soft-bodied tick, hook-worm, typhoid ('But I treated it the same as malaria, and got well') and an unidentified kidney complaint which he cured, apparently, simply by ignoring it. Following the same independent system he prefers bush dentistry without anaesthetic to any other variety, having had several teeth drawn by Africans as necessity arose. These details were brought out, not with pride, but to indicate without actually saying so that to try and persuade him to have his lungs screened was a waste of time. So I gave it up, not so much reassured as because he is a man totally unaccustomed to being nagged by women, and I did not wish to be the person identified in his memory with this lowering experience.

Instead we sat out on the rough grass near the frangipani, our feet upon empty chairs for want of a table, and followed the cautious manœuvres of a pair of bush-squirrels which lived in a hole in the bark of another tree and evidently thought that we would bear watching. First one round head and then another would appear in the hole, which was a tight fit, and when we had been still for a while the bolder of the two would come out and hang head down, splayed out on the rough bark like a flat skin, and watch us for long minutes with quivering gaze. Gradually they both became used to the spectacle and to our voices, and flitted about on the tree like a pair of shadows, no longer bolting for safety when Ionides coughed. His mind was running on Norman and his lion, for he guessed that he would be gone for many days, and convivially regretted him.

'It's a heart-breaking game,' he said, 'the Southern

Province has always been bad for man-eaters. Why, is a moot point; my own theory is that it's lack of their normal food, or difficulty in getting it. But once they're set in the habit they're remarkably adept and difficult to deal with. One receives a message that a man-eater's broken out somewhere, one gets to the place as quickly as possible —and the lion's gone. You wait for a week, ten days, a fortnight—no news. You've got a lot of other work to do—Game Wardens always have—and off you go. A few days later, back he comes, and picks off somebody else. It's very trying to the patience. They learn, you see, remarkably quickly; that's why it's desirable to get a man-eater early in his career, before he's developed tricks. Each time you fail to get an animal by a certain method—traps, driving, tracking and so on—he'll be much more alert for those methods in the future. They develop their own techniques. For instance, man being a diurnal animal who shuts himself up about four in the afternoon if there are lion about, these animals also frequently become diurnal, and actually hunt people working in the fields in broad daylight. Others prefer to rush them over the cooking-pots in the early evening. They change their natural habits in other ways, too. An experienced man-eater which has escaped after being hunted by various methods, learns, for instance, never to return to the kill. It eats a great whack of meat on the spot and then travels anything up to six to seven hours' walk before resting. If he's been scared by a trap, or escaped from one, it'll be very difficult to take him in a trap again. In fact it gets more and more difficult, with the lion profiting from experience all the time. I've known of one that was credited with ninety people before he was finally killed.'

'That was an opponent you could respect, surely? His record was comparable to your own.'

'A respectable record, certainly. Not too bad. My own technique with man-eaters, unconventional for the area, was to spread out my game-scouts, each with two local men with a drum, over a ten-mile radius. They had to circle each morning from one village to the next, looking for fresh tracks, while I camped at the point where the lion had been seen last. As soon as fresh track was found the man with the drum played the lion-call—two short beats and a long one, repeated—while the game-scout came back to my camp in case I hadn't heard. If it was early in the day, and the ground suitable, I didn't follow the lion-track until the sun was well up, to give him an opportunity to go to sleep. Then one just followed, often on hands and knees, through dense thicket, until one came up with the lion, which was often sleeping. Normally one got him then with a single shot. It's a more effective method than the usual *battu*, in which the lion gets alarmed and angry and people are often hurt, even shot on some occasions by their own pals.'

'Did you have much difficulty in getting this sort of help from unarmed people?'

'Not as a rule. They were willing enough to go with an armed game-scout. Certain tribes make difficulties, as they have to go through purification rites after a lion-killing, but one solved that by giving them the money to pay the witch-doctor. It wasn't too expensive.'

Ionides once lost one of his servants to a man-eater, and is thankful to remember that his hunting was not to blame. 'I'd been hunting this animal for ten days, in an area where the last victim had been a woman whom he'd taken just before I arrived. It so happened that this man of mine, my number-two orderly, had bought himself a new wife in the course of the journey, and asked my permission to leave the safari to take her back to his village. I was a little cross about it, because I needed him; however, I said, "Very well, take the bloody woman back," so off he went, and I heard no more about him for several days. But what happened was this. They spent two nights in a village on the way to Tunduru, near where I'd shot an elephant on the way out; the last I ever shot, as a matter of fact, because it was doing so much damage to crops and there was no game-scout near. The carcase was still there, just rotting skin and bones. The village people advised him not to sleep outside since there were lion in the area, but to come into one of the huts. But this man said no, and he and his woman slept on a *kitanda*—African string bed—under a lean-to of thatch. Now, unknown to him, his track had been followed all the way by this same lion, the one I was after; whether deliberately following him or simply going on the same track, nobody knows. On the second night the people in the hut heard a thud outside, where the man and his wife were sleeping. They at once called out, and the woman replied, "My husband is not here; he must have gone to urinate." She had been asleep, you see. But they were not satisfied, and came out with torches lit from the fire, and found blood on the ground. They took the woman inside and next morning found that the lion had left the body of her husband in the grass with a great bite through the back of the head, and was lying under a tree about fifteen yards away, watching them. They were unarmed, and very frightened, and next morning there was nothing left of the man but the head. They then managed to get hold of some game-scouts—I was a long way off by then, in another district altogether—and by luck the lion was lying up by the carcase of the elephant, chewing the old skin, and the scouts were able to get him on the second day. I saw the skin afterwards, an adult lion in the prime of life, perfect teeth, no apparent reason for man-eating. Yet he must have been at it for a good while, for my servant was the forty-fifth known victim.'

But going after man-eaters, though a necessary part of his work in the past, is not a thing that Ionides ever enjoyed, since one cannot be choosey in one's methods and must often transgress what he calls the ethics of hunting. These ethics are based on the notion that hunting is a contest in which every animal must be given a reasonable chance, an idea which becomes sentimental with a too dangerous quarry. One of the first symptoms that he noticed in himself, when he began to change from a blood-thirsty hunter into a naturalist, was that he had daydreams of going back to spears and arrows, so as to feel 'more comfortable'. As skill increased dissatisfaction grew, and he experienced pleasure only when hunting was difficult. As to those modern organized safaris in which people slaughter animals from motor-cars, his loathing and indignation make him speechless; the only subject, perhaps, capable of doing so.

*

The first sight of Mafia, dark with coconut palms and ringed with every conceivable colour of the ocean (translucent green on the reefs, changing abruptly to a blue so deep that it was almost purple) was so magical after the dry monotony of the plateau as to seem like an hallucination. Other islands, small and densely wooded, lay to the seaward side, and farther out the drowned shadows of coral formations still far below the surface. We came down into warm air which we breathed gratefully, a heat that caressed the skin without oppressing, perpetually stirring and alive with the breath of the sea. And there on the airstrip, with a Land Rover waiting, was a slight man with a nautical beard, our celebrated fisherman. He and Ionides fell into conversation at once, and the twenty-mile drive to the fishing-club, slow and bewildering, over a narrow and rutted sandy road which took innumerable turns and dived into little streams without warning, was spent in a close inquiry into the possibility of pythons and the arrangements that had been made for our accommodation. The most likely places, it seemed, were at the north end of the island, which was covered with copra plantations and mostly uninhabited, and here our friend had been able to borrow a house. It had only just been built, he said, and belonged to an enterprising character who intended to make his permanent home in the island, but who was at present in Kenya. There were two servants belonging to the place, and he thought we would be comfortable. In the meantime he had sent out word all over the island that python news was wanted. The snakes were certainly there, but he feared that the islanders' lethargy might defeat us. They were different, it appeared, from the Makonde people; something to do with the climate, no doubt; they were resolutely idle. Rewards, strange to say, had little effect; they were not interested in money. This is a great problem for the island, which depends for its economy on copra and needs a constant labour force for the plantations. The Mafia people will work for as much as a week, but as soon as pay-day is over they disappear, and for years it has been customary to import seasonal labour from the Makonde Plateau. This struck us as ominous, and Ionides became silent. If we had failed to hear of a python from the Makonde, to whom money is sacred, how should we fare on Mafia, where nobody wanted it? He was further disturbed, when we arrived at the fishing-club, by the loss of his favourite snake-stick, which had been tied on the roof of the car and was unaccountably missing. Somewhere in that twenty miles of bush this faithful and long-used tool had somehow escaped, and he was sceptical of Swann's assurances that it would be found tomorrow. It was an evil omen.

After a night in the comfortable thatched cabins of the fishing-club and fortified by a delicious breakfast we set about preparations for our small journey. I had wakened before sunrise and gone down in the early light to the narrow beach to swim out to one of the fishing-boats belonging to the club, a blunt little launch with a roofed-in superstructure on which big-game fishermen, when they came, presumably sat, casting their heavy lines for tarpon and marlin. The tide ran strongly and carried me out of my course to a further spit, where a solitary African woman was modestly bathing in her *kanga* in shallow water. The sea was pearly, and as the tide carried me buoyantly along the sun came up in a blaze on the horizon, turning the sea to gold so that I had to close my eyes to the blinding rays. I had never seen the sunrise so, watching from the arms of the sea, and the sense of magic and miracle was so strong that it was like being a part of the elements on the morning of creation.

Practical problems, once I had dressed and returned, brought me to my senses. A guide had been hired for the thirty-mile journey to our new home, and an ancient Land Rover found which we might borrow. This, since Ionides will not drive unless his life depends on it, was to be my charge, and I inspected the thing with apprehension, oppressed by ignorance and responsibility. If anything went wrong I should be helpless, and our guide, an elderly African, was no mechanic. It was only by chance that I noticed there was no spare wheel. This caused a delay when the luggage and boxes of food had already been stowed, but not even the thought of a python could make me so reckless as to go without one; and after a time a spare was disinterred from a distant out-house, an extremely ancient specimen to be sure, with the comb of a wasp's nest built between two of the spokes, but presumably usable. We set off gingerly over the sandy grass, rattling with boxes and age and cans of petrol.

True to its sterling nature the vehicle went well enough, though shakily, and my only moment of horror was when I found it had no brakes. This was borne in on us only after two or three miles, for the island was perfectly flat and the soft sand of the road would have made speed impossible if I had had a mind for it; but the track was crossed at intervals by small streams which through time had worn their way into steep gullies, and it was through braking on the slope of the first that I discovered the deficiency. We cannoned down to the water at twenty miles an hour and rushed up the opposite slope on our own impetus, the foot-brake pressed down to the floor boards and the handbrake convulsively jumping in my left hand. After that we went even more slowly and cautiously than before, changing to bottom gear at the first hint of a declivity and grinding up the far side with shuddering effort. Our guide laughed happily at each of these performances and Ionides preserved a calm for which I was grateful, but the drive, in spite of the beauty of the copra plantations, the lushness of vegetation and our occasional dazzling glimpses of the sea, was a mixed pleasure. We mistook our way several times, the track branching occasionally in two directions and every turn looking bafflingly the same; but as fast as I took the wrong turn our guide recollected himself, so that at last we were on the long, straight, uncomplicated track leading to our destination. The sea appeared, we heard the drone of the surf, and the road petered out among the rocks and palm-trees of a little promontory.

This promontory—Ras Mbizi, the cape of the diver—was one horn of a shallow bay, stretching away to the left for perhaps a mile, a strip of sand between palm-trees and the sea, the perfect vision, so long imagined and for once magically true, of a coral island. The promontory itself was an outcrop of coral rock, as dead and pitted as cinders, on which a fringe of coconut palms had found a footing, and here, by a rare and romantic stroke, a thatched house had been hidden in the shade. We climbed out and eagerly examined our new home. The house was like none I had ever seen or imagined; barely finished, built for one man to live in, it was so cunningly placed under the palms within its bastion of rock that if one walked a few paces away, in any direction, it disappeared from sight. The tide was full when we first saw it, with the sea lapping softly at the foot of the rocks which framed our view of the ocean like a broken wall, through which coconut palms and mangroves had spread their roots. Behind the house, beyond the thatch of the servants' huts and the little cook-house, the copra plantation closed in with the density of forest. The beach could be seen only by going through the trees and scrambling through rocks at the edge of the promontory, where the long perspective of coral sand began, an empty and exquisite curve on which nothing stirred. The house itself was a simple rectangle, thickly thatched, with a deep and cool veranda. There were two main rooms, each with a smaller one behind it, and the enchantment of the design was in the walls, which were breast-high, the rest of the space being filled with mosquito netting. Thus, when one stepped inside and closed the door, one was still in the open; there was a bed, a writing-desk and a book-case, but the trees were still around one on two sides, and on the third were rock-framed vistas of the ocean. It was not private, certainly; it was more like an elegant aviary than a house; but privacy would have been dearly bought with walls. From my bedroom, as I unpacked, I could see across the intervening veranda to Ionides in his; our host's two African servants went to and fro beyond the netting, delicately not looking, and one had the feeling of preparing to camp in the utmost comfort and almost wholly in the open. Behind my bedroom was a bathroom with walls, a new bath and wash-basin and—O luxury!—running water. This water could even be heated by an outside stove; I could already hear the crackling of new-lit wood. Behind Ionides' bedroom was a store-room where food was kept, and beyond that, nothing. The veranda ran from front to back, like an open living-room, and here a wooden table was set and two canvas chairs, and a couple of packing-cases to put our feet on. When we had explored and exclaimed, inspected each other's bedrooms and turned on the taps, we were still not quite at an end of the domestic glories, for the lavatory was at a little distance from the house and was in itself memorable. Wedged into the rocks and partly overhanging the sea was a little cabin the size of a telephone booth, which, when the door was opened, transformed itself into a belvedere, for there was no fourth wall. One sat in perfect seclusion gazing at the sea, or even when the tide was out at the endless gleaming expanse of living reef. It was the final poetic detail of a house planned for peace and contemplation, set in a place of such spellbound solitude that even on this first day the thought of leaving it brought a melancholy pang.

But we had come for pythons, and as the days went by without news I was almost ashamed that Ionides should see me so happy. He refused to stir from the house, sitting from sunrise till night on the veranda, alert for the footfall of a messenger who never came. But I could not be so resolute. The water was deep and warm when the tide was full, swirling in with an ocean surge to engulf the rocks, and when it was low, withdrawn to a wisp of breakers a mile away, the shallow mysterious country of the reef drew me with a curiosity that no sense of the purpose of our being there could coerce me to resist. This was my first coral island, first reef, first teeming and tropical sea, and not even the hope of a python, nor Ionides' stoical patience in the shade of the house, could keep me for more than an hour or two away from it.

The first time I escaped along the beach, promising, in case of news, to stay within earshot of Ionides' bellow, I experienced what I took to be an optical illusion. The sun was hot and the light extremely dazzling, and as I stepped down on the warm sand the whole surface of the beach appeared to move. I stood still. After a quivering moment the movement ceased. It was not the sand that had stirred, but thousands and thousands of pearly crabs, pale and transparent as ghosts, fleeing on the tips of their toes at my approach. They watched me come and retreated as an army, keeping strategic distance, and when I quickened my pace they either ran into the edge of the sea or scrambled out of sight down their sandy burrows. The whole expanse of sand, still firm from the tide, was mined all over with tunnels freshly dug, each one with a pile of sand at some distance from the mouth, to which the methodical creatures transported their debris. These ghost crabs, so nimble and watchful, advancing and retreating in waves all over the sand, were the first I saw, but I found when I sat very still and the hordes returned that they were only a part of an infinitely various population. Periscope crabs, projecting their eyes on stalks from the mouths of their burrows, crept out at length and attended to their affairs, excavating with the frantic haste of creatures aware there is not a moment to be lost, hunting for sand-flies in the sea-refuse, chasing one another off their chosen terrain and occasionally sitting down as though to consider, the base of the square carapace resting on the sand, polished claws held alertly before them. In this posture they assumed a curiously bat-like aspect, the periscope eyes jutting up for ears and the angular spread of the legs simulating wings. Their colours were delicate, some bleached and white as a scoured sea-shell, some pearly pink, others a tender green. A pair came very close, maintaining a cautious distance from me as from one another, and hunted for food on either side of my feet. The pink crab was after flies, but without success, stalking his prey with caution and open claws, making mad rushes which ended each time in hairbreadth miscalculation; the green one, more experienced or less ambitious, was carefully turning over some weedy jetsam, both claws cramming fragmentary findings into his trap-door mouth. When at length I moved, the hordes retreated as before, fleeing along the beach like leaves in the wind and scampering in little flurries into the sea. What happened to them when the tide came in I never discovered, though I suspect they exchanged one element for another, busily scouring the sea-floor while their sand-castles crumbled, waiting only for the moment when the beach was theirs again and they could resume their endless work of digging and tunnelling.

If I were a believer in astrology, knowing myself born under the Crab, the Moon my planet and the sea, old friend and enemy, my element, what magical portents and prophecies might I not have deduced from those unforgettable days and nights on Mafia! The moon was almost at the full and grandly clear, silvering the thatch of the house each night and throwing shadows of palm-trees over the sand with a soft brilliance only less luminous than day. The sea was around us always, drowning the rocks or withdrawn to the fringe of the reef, where it kept up a far-away roar like the voice of a shell, leaving milky shallows by day in which I wandered entranced, stooping to peer, to touch, to examine among the innumerable living strangenesses inhabiting the reef. The crabs were everywhere, but there were other grotesque shapes that I mistrusted; creatures of nightmare, attenuated star-fish or sea-spiders, I could not guess which, spreading mahogany-dark limbs like tentacles and in places so densely massed that at first I walked through them boldly, taking the quavering growth for a thicket of weed. But the tentacles stirred at my touch, flinching and coiling, and I had a moment of panic as I splashed a hasty retreat into clearer water. Others were blue and slate-coloured, delicately striped, rayed out on the floor of the sea like reflected stars; and there were monstrous things like caterpillars seen through the microscope, soft to the touch, huge as rolling-pins, buff, pink, and green, covered with spiny warts. But the tribes of crabs were masters of this wilderness, and as weedy islands of rock were uncovered by the ebb and increased and ran together in slippery continents, I was pursued by sounds which at first I could not interpret, for all the world like the smacking of lips and the popping of corks—the noises of crabs exchanging mysterious signals all over the reef. The reef-crabs were very different from those opalescent ones, those spiders made of pearl that I had watched on the beach; red and sturdy, they sat with folded arms in hollows of the rock, raising their claws in menace as I approached, and once or twice, with startling effrontery, squirting a jet of water over my legs. The most beautiful of all were cerulean blue, larger and more lightly built than the others, retreating through shallow water, tip-toeing nimbly backwards with arms outspread, dodging away from my shadow like wary boxers. I could not catch them though I repeatedly tried; they were not to be taken by surprise, always mockingly facing me and out of reach, dancing away under water with open claws. There were other treasures, though, to be taken from the rocks, huge cowries richly mottled and smooth as glass, lying like turkeys' eggs in a slimy nest, and these were dislodged with a sucking noise, while the tender membrane which covered them ran back at my touch and became a cringing frill of slippery flesh. The shells living and dead, infinitely various in colour and fantasy, polished, fluted, convoluted, spined, were irresistible, and at first I gathered more than I could carry; but sooner or later conscience would begin to stir, I would guiltily measure the mile or more I had wandered, knowing that I had long been out of sight and sound of our promontory, and begin to splash my way back to the hidden house.

I covered the last stretch of beach with apprehension, always afraid I should find Ionides gone, sped off to some swampy place after his python, for I was under no delusion that I should be waited for. But he was always there as I had left him, strewing the sand with cigarette-ends, brooding on the feckless habits of the islanders, considering fresh strategies. I began to fear, and he already knew, that the week we had allowed ourselves would end as it had begun, and that we should go away empty-handed. On the last day, he said bitterly, when the aeroplane was due, we should hear of a python, and by then, as we might have guessed, it would be too late. So we spent our last evenings in talk, sitting in a circle of lamplight on the veranda, watching the swooping bats and the fireflies and consoling ourselves with daydream plans for the future.

Our favourite scheme, absorbing because there were rough maps to be sketched and lists made of minimum equipment, was that the following year we should make a safari into the Selous Reserve, which Ionides knew from the years he had spent there as a Game Ranger, and which still remains one of the few virgin areas of Africa. Frederick

Courteney Selous is one of Ionides' heroes, whose life in some ways has foreshadowed the pattern of his own. Selous, too, was at Rugby, and from boyhood had a passion for wild life which carried him to Africa, where, among other distinctions, he became known as the greatest hunter of all time; a title he deprecated, preferring to be remembered as a naturalist. In the First World War he returned to Tanganyika, then German East Africa, and was killed there. He is buried not many miles from Liwale, Ionides' first home, in the wild country which is now a game reserve and commemorates his name. One day, if all goes well with Tanganyika, roads will be made into this huge territory, the tsetse fly perhaps will be controlled, and organized safaris bring a rich tourist revenue into the country. This is not a prospect that Ionides regards with pleasure, for he likes to think that here at least, in a territory as rich in wild life as any in Africa, the tsetse fly, carrier of sleeping-sickness, has made continued human habitation impossible. The villages have been cleared out long ago by the government, and apart from Game Department inspection and control the animals have it to themselves, as unchecked and unmolested as in the days before the first tribes moved into it. The balance of nature, an unfashionable concept nowadays except under its new name of ecological equilibrium, but one which Ionides continues to believe in, maintains itself in the absence of man with all its old extravagant success, and he likes to think that the mosquito and the tsetse fly flourish there with the rest, and that no species is exterminated.

'I don't quite know what they mean,' he said, on our last night at Ras Mbizi, 'when they claim that the old idea of the balance of nature is fallacious. What I do know is this: that in remote areas, uncivilized man, predators, and the animals that are preyed on—carnivora and herbivora—have all contrived to live together without terrible damage to any of the three. The carnivora, the predators, act as a natural normal check on the herbivora. As to man—with whom in these days we're so tenderly concerned—he'll lose an odd cow or an odd goat from time to time; possibly a man-eater will take one or two of his people, and afterwards the man-eater will be hunted down and killed. He stands to lose a certain amount of his crops to pigs, baboons, elephants and other crop-raiding animals. But I've never heard of a case of the human animal suffering *unduly* when what I still call the balance of nature has been kept. If, on the other hand, as has happened in Africa comparatively recently, the carnivora are destroyed or nearly destroyed (since the price of leopard-skins went up, you know, leopards have been very much reduced), the smaller so-called vermin, pigs, baboons and monkeys, have caused the most unheard-of damage to crops, owing to the disappearance of their natural check, which is the leopard. And to a certain degree the lion. For this reason one should be very cautious about organizing the wholesale killing of any species on the ground of its alleged damage to human beings. I find it very repugnant when I hear officials of various departments adopting the attitude that man is the lord of creation, and that every other animal which may do the slightest apparent damage to him must therefore be exterminated for his convenience.'

We were sitting on the veranda in the brief dusk, the lamp still unlit, and from time to time great bats, flying high and steadily like homing cormorants, passed over on their nightly journey to the island of Chole, where ripe bananas drop to the ground among the tree-choked ruins of the fort which is all that remains of the German administration. 'Fruit-eating bats,' he said, raising his eyes appreciatively as they went over, '*Eidolon helvum*, probably. Nobody's yet thought of exterminating *them*, fortunately.' But he is pessimistic about the survival of wild life in Africa, in spite of all the money and propaganda now being deployed to that end; in his opinion twenty years too late. 'Nowadays, owing to the advance of medicine and other forms of progress, the human animal is breeding more and more prolifically, taking up more and more land, making ever more exhausting demands on the country, and it is certainly true that on highly cultivated land man in great numbers cannot live together with the larger forms of wild life. Therefore it looks as though the wild life is doomed to go.'

'What solution would you suggest, then, if you had power to enforce it?'

'Reduce the number of human beings, *drastically.*'

'And how would you do that, pray?'

'I can't think of any method that you would approve of, unfortunately, but I personally have a great faith in nature. I have an idea that, given time, she will adjust matters very well. Just as some other animals have become extinct, for some reasons we know and some we don't, so it seems to me quite possible that ever since the days of the industrial revolution man has been working up a situation which must end with his extinction.'

'You mean the bomb?'

'Possibly. Or some as yet unknown disease, caused by over-crowding. It's difficult to prophesy. But even if there were wide-spread atomic war it seems to me more likely that small pockets of human animals would continue to exist in out-of-the-way places. Having lost their modern implements and run out of ammunition and so on they would revert, I think, to pure survival and become like any other mammal—in which case it would take them a very long time indeed to become so prolific again, if they were ever able to.'

From the look on his face, suddenly visible as the house-boy appears from the dark with a hurricane lamp, one can see that such a reversal would not dismay him, and I found myself wondering afresh, as so often before, how he privately justifies his life as a hunter when the extermination of any species enrages him.

'But hunting and extermination are quite different. I look at it in this way. I am a carnivorous animal living mainly on meat. I have strongly developed in me the ordinary hunting instinct which is dormant or present, to a certain extent, in most human animals. And hunting—I mean *proper* hunting—never seriously hurts a species because the whole essence of the thing is for it to be so difficult that very few animals are killed. Beyond that I don't attempt to justify it. But wholesale slaughter, extermination, wasteful killing, especially when done on the grounds of some alleged principle, I consider very damaging. Nor do I think it accords at all with normal hunting instincts, which are natural and healthy. The conclusion I come to, I think, is this—that until we know much more than anybody does at present I would not willingly agree to the extermination of any creature whatever, not even the malarial mosquito.'

'Nor the tsetse fly?'

'No. Because a worse thing might happen. We don't yet know all the functions these animals may perform. I would reduce them, kill them out in certain areas, I agree; but irrevocably exterminate them, no. If we only knew it, the malarial mosquito and the sleeping-sickness tsetse fly are two of our greatest friends. Many's the place they have preserved from foul exploitation.'

'Like the Selous Reserve?'

'Yes, so far, thank God. Long may it continue.'

*

True to Ionides' prophecy, when we had packed our boxes and gear and rattled away at last from Ras Mbizi, we were met at the fishing-club by a man who had come by canoe from the island of Juani with news, so he claimed, of a python of huge proportions holed up in a rock. It needed only this to send Ionides off to his cabin in speechless annoyance, for of course it was too late. The plane was due next day which would take us to Dar-es-Salaam, and even if the news were true (which he doubted, not liking the man's replies to his close questions) it might well take a week of camping and watching to prove it. There was nothing left but to spend our last day as pleasantly as we could, and this we did with Swann in one of his fishing-boats, prowling about over the coral-heads beyond the fringe of the reef, and occasionally dropping anchor into one of them so that I could swim. Swann is a fisherman of genius, not a swimmer, and Ionides sat sedately in the middle of the boat, wearing a lady's raffia hat which had been found for him at the club (the sun was very hot) and in which he contrived to look both dashing and correct. But to me the day passed as an extraordinary dream, idling face downwards on the water above a spectacle so brilliant and bizarre that I could not believe what my astonished eyes took in, and continually came back to the boat for reassurance. The coral bloomed in every imaginable shape and colour, sprouting from what might have been the towers of some legendary submerged cathedral, and rising and falling through this rainbow forest, streaming in glistening droves from the deep water, hunting through rocky arches and darting into crevices, were the gaudiest and most improbable fish that I had ever imagined. No shape, no stripe, no dazzling design of daffodil and violet was too strange for them to have put on for protection or allure, and I clung to the coral pinnacles until my lungs were bursting. But there were no sea-snakes nor any likelihood of any, and except for a few courteous glances over the side, through a glass-bottomed box, Ionides spent the blazing hours in the shade of the boat's superstructure, eating a little fish when it was caught and cooked, feeding the moving tide with the debris of smoking, wrapped up in unusual silence, peacefully contemplating.

Our solitary interlude was at an end, and when next morning we found ourselves in Dar-es-Salaam, being met at the airport by Ionides' cronies, I was reminded of the day when I had first seen him on Waterloo Station, standing grave, remarkable and detached in an ordinary crowd which heightened his own extraordinariness to an extreme. The only difference was that in London I had come on him alone, whereas now he was welcomed on every hand as a rare and auspicious migrant, so that we were swept away on a wave of merry hospitality which revealed him in a not altogether unsuspected aspect as the most gregarious of men. There were occasions, for which he was amiably though not too willingly smartened up; a respectable jacket and trousers were borrowed for a handsome evening at the Dar-es-Salaam Club (the trousers held up for the most part with a free hand, since no other man's garments can be trusted to keep a reliable grip on his bones), his hair and jersey were washed with delightful results, Ionides accommodating himself to everyone's wishes until the final point was reached of offering him a tie. The tie was rejected with passion, as everyone expected; even for dining out in the capital one must not push him too far. (A willing audience of this partial transformation, I remembered with pleasure that Sir Richard Turnbull, the outgoing Governor, had told me how touched he had been on an occasion when Ionides had stayed at Government House and had so far compromised his principles as to provide himself with a dinner-jacket and tie and even patent-leather pumps, which he would never have suspected he possessed; little knowing that these garments had been urgently lent half an hour before dinner by his own scandalized A.D.C.)

The days slipped by as I waited for my flight to Rome, days divided between the comings and goings of friends (the cheerful nickname 'Iodine' on everyone's lips, this being only too obviously what everyone has called him since his schooldays, though I never quite got used to it), our long late-night conferences on his coming cobra-safari, and our own plans for a trek into the Selous. All too soon the final day arrived, when, to please me rather than himself, since his mind was already dwelling on Egyptian cobra, we made a brief sentimental excursion to Bagamoyo.

Bagamoyo, decaying Arab town on the beach from which so many of the great explorers began their journeys, where Burton, Speke and Stanley landed from heavy dhows from Zanzibar and began the long wrangle for stores and porters, is a perfect if melancholy place for saying goodbye. It is a dying village now, with crumbling Arab tombs in the yellow grass and the bleached bones of ships sticking up from the sand. Nothing happens there any more, and the long single street, lined with flaking plaster houses from which the heavy doors, once gorgeous with brass and carving in the days of Arab prosperity, have nearly all fallen or been carried away, is sad with the emptiness of a merchants' street which trade has deserted. Only in one humble shop, a silversmith's, was there a sign that some kind of craft was still carried on; a few shoddy bracelets and ear-rings of Indian silver were spread out in display; but when we went inside, hoping to buy some trinket to mark the occasion, the old man who crept out from the gloom had nothing further to show. He made nothing nowadays, he said; these few gimcrack ornaments were his sole stock-in-trade, and his listless air suggested small hope of selling them. But some life goes on; the fishing continues, as it must always have done since before the Arabs came; and on the shore we were offered dangling bunches of fish and a slimy basket of octopus which was still less to our purpose. It is a place dwindled by time into a scene for endings rather than beginnings; even the stone which marks the spot from which Burton and Speke set off on their last journey leaves one with a curious feeling of unbelief.

Yet the name of Bagamoyo still has power, recalling those dark engravings in shabby volumes of African exploration which have sown a seed of longing in many an unwary child, and which, remembering the forgotten bookcase in my grandfather's house, I saw again as I stood on the beach with Ionides, presenting themselves with a strangely familiar air, as though my being there at all, even the presence of my dear Ionides himself, were facts for which they might be held responsible.

GOD'S APOLOGY
A Chronicle of Three Friends

Richard Ingrams

In this very entertaining book, Richard Ingrams celebrates the friendship of three men: Hugh Kingsmill, writer and former literary editor of *Punch*, Hesketh Pearson, the biographer, and Malcolm Muggeridge. At the centre of the group was Kingsmill, whose lack of success as a writer was perhaps a result of his memorable success as a conversationalist and friend. The portrait that Richard Ingrams draws of the relationship between the three men is affectionate and compelling. In the words of Kingsmill: 'Friends are God's apology for relations.'

'Most readable and spirited. . . . A book that is so full of affection is most welcome nowadays.' Nigel Dennis, *Sunday Telegraph*

BEYOND FRONTIERS

Jasper Parrott with Vladimir Ashkenazy

Vladimir Ashkenazy is known throughout the world as one of the greatest pianiests of our time. Despite his fame he is a very private man, but his experiences as a child prodigy under the Soviet system and his subsequent emigration to the West have affected so profoundly his views about music, politics and people that this book has grown out of his wish to share these thoughts with others – to communicate in a medium other than music.

'. . . a far cry from the usual collection of amiable anecdotes surrounding the life of a virtuoso. Instead, it is an examination of the thoughts, musical and political, of a great artist, written with intelligence, wit, and even wisdom.' André Previn

THE DRAGON EMPRESS

Marina Warner

From 1861 to 1908, the Empress Dowager Tz'u-hsi dominated China. In this immensely readable biography, Marina Warner lays bare Tz'u-hsi's complex personality, and portrays a China in rapid decline as poverty, civil war and foreign exploitation and invasion brought about the fall of the Ch'ing dynasty.

'A fresh and fascinating account that reveals China's last imperial reign as surely the most absurd government ever to have had charge of a major nation. I read every word.' Barbara W. Tuchman

THE GREAT HUNGER

Cecil Woodham-Smith

'A moving and terrible book. It combines great literary power with great learning. It explains much in modern Ireland and in modern America.' D. W. Brogan

The Great Hunger is the story of one of the worst disasters of all time: the Irish potato famine of the eighteen-forties during which more than a million people died. In her balanced and dispassionate story, Cecil Woodham-Smith traces the suffering, courage, blundering stupidity and tragedy whose effects on the history of Ireland, the United States and England are still visible more than a hundred years later.